THE SECRET APARTMENT

THE

SECRET

APARTMENT

Natalie Fast

delacorte press

Published by
Delacorte Press
an imprint of
Random House Children's Books
a division of Random House, Inc.
New York

Produced by Alloy Entertainment
151 West 26th Street
New York, New York 10001

ALLOY
ENTERTAINMENT

Visit us on the Web! www.randomhouse.com/kids
Educators and librarians, for a variety of teaching tools, visit us at
www.randomhouse.com/teachers

Library of Congress Cataloging-in-Publication Data
Fast, Natalie.
The secret apartment / Natalie Fast.
p. cm.
Summary: New to New York City, eleven-year-old Jillian makes friends, spies on
her neighbors across the street, and solves a mystery.
ISBN 0-385-74671-7 (Hardcover)—ISBN 0-385-90902-0 (Library binding)
[1. Moving, Household—Fiction. 2. Remarriage—Fiction. 3. Grief—Fiction.
4. New York (N.Y.)—Fiction. 5. Mystery and detective stories.] I. Title.
PZ7.F266Se 2005
[Fic]—dc22   2004030948

The text of this book is set in 12.5-point Minion.

Book design by Angela Carlino

Printed in the United States of America

October 2005

10 9 8 7 6 5 4 3 2 1

BVG

ME
(...in disguise)

big knife

stinky cheese

Kaputsa's angry cheese man!

1

"Jillian, don't hold your nose like that," my mother scolded, nudging me. "It's rude."

I was standing next to my mom at the cheese counter at Kaputsa's—the fanciest grocery store in all of New York City's Upper West Side—and I felt a little icky.

"But it *smells*," I complained.

"This is *Kaputsa's*," she hissed. "A very famous grocery store! Their cheese does not smell."

I snorted. Some famous grocery store. They didn't

even sell normal food here—only aisles and aisles of creepy, blobby, hairy vegetables that looked more like science experiments than things you could eat. I wanted to go home to Pennsylvania, to a normal grocery store, with normal food in it.

"This is the best cheese counter in the city," my mother murmured as we waited our turn. She pointed to an oozy pile in the glass case. "Those cheeses there are the exotic cheeses. They will be perfect for the party tonight."

She was making a huge deal out of this party she and my new stepfather, Michael, were throwing. It was her first big New York party, she'd explained, and she wanted to do it up right. She was never this way when we lived in Pennsylvania, or when she was with my dad, who died of cancer two and a half years before. I slumped my shoulders down even farther. I wished I was a puddle on the floor so someone at Kaputsa's could come and mop me up.

"Next!" roared a voice. Behind the foul-smelling cheese counter stood a man who honestly looked like he should have been in the circus. He was very tall, like maybe he was on stilts, except he wasn't, and he had a pitted face and a giant handlebar mustache. His eyes were small and beady, and his mouth curled down in a frown. He wore a purple and white striped Kaputsa's apron and hat; in his left hand he was jangling a bunch of keys, and in his right hand he held a long, thin knife, like some really evil jailkeeper.

"Yikes," I said. "They let that scary guy work here?"

"Shhh," my mother said to me. "Try to behave."

It was my second day in New York City. My mom and I had just moved there, to a really dark and spooky building called the Dakota, on Seventy-second Street. It had all seemed like a blur. One minute, I was sitting on my blue bedspread in Pennsylvania, doodling a T-shirt design for this boy I liked, thinking that maybe he liked me, too. Next minute, my mom's in a wedding gown, and I'm in an itchy lime green lacy bridesmaid dress, allergic to the flowers and sneezing like crazy.

Michael, my brand-new stepfather, owned a huge publishing company in New York, so he couldn't just leave it behind to move to Pennsylvania. He made the move easier for my mom by setting her up with a really great new editor job at *Savvy*, one of his coolest magazines. She was happy, but I had to leave my bedroom and all my friends in Pennsylvania behind. It really stank, and not just because of all the cheese.

"Things will get better," my mom had assured me. "New York just takes some getting used to." But how would she know? She'd only been here for a day too!

"Should I get Coach Farm triple cream, or Taleggio, or both?" my mother murmured.

I guess you could say it was all Michael's fault that we were there. After my dad died, my mother dated a couple of other guys, but Michael was different. My only opinion of him was that he had really large fleshy ears. And, oh yeah, he had a funny accent from somewhere. Later, my mother told me it was Australia.

I squirmed around, leaning against the Kaputsa's counter, missing things. I missed my friends and the boy, Dan Connelly, I had a crush on. I even missed Harry, the obnoxious nine-year-old who lived next door and once came after me, blindfolded, carrying his mom's garden hoe. The night before, as I listened to the traffic whoosh down Central Park West, six stories below me, I'd wished I could stick my tongue out at Harry just one more time.

And I missed my father more than ever. He used to make me pancakes, take me sledding, and draw cartoons of my mom and me. I wondered if my mom even thought about him anymore.

"Stop wasting my time! What do you want?" the cheese seller shouted, waving the knife. I noticed that his little purple and white nametag said JACQUES. He took the key chain he was jangling and placed it behind the counter.

"Oh, well, I'm not sure," my mother said, her hand on her cheek. "I'm having a dinner party tonight, and I was thinking the Manchego, but—"

"Manchego would be terrible for a dinner party!" Jacques roared. "Get Brie! Brie is the best! Only Brie!"

This guy needed to chill out. He had an accent. French, maybe. I bet he ate a lot of cheese.

"Brie, I'm telling you!" Jacques bossed my mother.

"But I don't know if everyone likes Brie . . . ," my mother said.

Jacques gave an impatient little sigh.

I decided to take a look around. I saw a tall spindly woman wearing black leggings and a black T-shirt, peering into a nearby pickle barrel. She was leaning so far over that her head was almost completely inside. "Emily, hold the basket," the woman squealed. "I'm searching for just the right pickle."

A girl, about my age—eleven, going into sixth grade—took the woman's shopping basket. She wore a bright blue boa draped around her shoulders and cool blue Puma sneakers on her feet. She kept flinging the end of the boa around so that it brushed against the cheese display and the olive barrels. She looked about as miserable as I was. She caught my gaze and rolled her eyes at her mom's back. Then she pointed at a hunk of wrapped cheese and stuck out her tongue and pinched her nose.

I giggled. She seemed nice and fun. I needed to make friends in New York. I might as well start now.

I had begun to move in the girl's direction when it happened.

I could be clumsy sometimes, and as I stepped forward, my feet went out from under me. I tried to catch myself on one of the tables that displayed the bricks of cheese, but my hand slipped. I felt the table start to give as I went sprawling onto the checkerboard floor.

A split second later, the table completely collapsed, raining bricks of cheese down on me!

"Jillian!" I heard my mother shout. "Are you all right?"

"Look out!" I cried. Cheese was rolling everywhere.

A hunk skidded right under a woman's heel. But she didn't see it and let out a scream and went sprawling!

"Jillian, get up!" my mother said, standing over me.

As the woman fell, she grabbed the side of another cheese table, and it began to collapse just like mine had! Gooey white mounds of cheese cascaded to the ground. When they hit the floor, they bounced! Some of them bounced really high into the air, like they were made of rubber.

"Ahhh!" a man screamed, trying to get out of the way of the bouncing cheese. But the cheese got underneath his feet anyway and tripped him up. The contents of his basket—avocados, bananas, rice in a sack—went flying. More people screamed.

I didn't know whether to laugh or cry. But then I got a look at my mom's horrified face.

"Get off the floor right this instant!" she said through her teeth.

I quickly pushed myself up. The cheese guy was still behind the counter, hopping up and down like a monkey. The key around his neck bounced and kept slapping him on the chest. "You! Girl who ruined all my cheese! And mother of the girl who ruined all my cheese! Get out of my section!"

"You don't own the cheese section!" I said. "You can't just throw us out."

"Jillian!" my mother whispered.

Jacques stamped his foot. His face was getting redder and redder by the minute. The tips of his mustache were quivering. He stamped his foot again and pounded his fist on the glass-topped counter. He stepped back, bumping into a large shelf of cheese behind the counter. "Uh-oh," I said. A giant wheel of cheese balanced on the top shelf began to teeter. A few seconds later, it fell. Right on his head.

But it didn't end there. The big cheese started another massive chain reaction. Little cheeses, stacked high on the shelf above him, began to rain down on his noggin. *"Alors!"* he cried. He swung his arms around, trying to swat the cheese away. Other shoppers had stopped and were laughing or gawking or tripping over all the cheese on the floor.

"This is so embarrassing," my mother whispered. "We have to leave."

"Hey, did you plan that?" asked a voice behind me.

I turned around. It was the girl with the boa and the Pumas. I grinned.

"Not exactly," I said.

"But it was so cool!" she whispered, her eyes widening. "It was the most exciting thing I've seen at Kaputsa's ever! And I've been coming here since I was a baby!"

"Do you live near here?" I asked.

"Yeah," she said. "I'm Emily."

"I'm Jillian," I said.

"Jillian," came my mother's voice. "I'm leaving. Right now."

"I have to find my mom anyway," Emily said. "She's probably in the gourmet meat section." She stuck her tongue out. "Blech."

"See you around," I said to Emily, giving her a disappointed smile.

"Bye," she called.

At that, my mom grabbed me by the upper arm and dragged me out of Kaputsa's.

blown-out hair

cell phone (ALWAYS ringing)

Mariella ... my EVIL stepsister!

Along the sidewalk, all sorts of stuff were for sale: socks, underwear, old paperback books. I noticed one called *Picasso's Blue Period,* and paused to look.

"Honey." My mother stopped. "We don't have time."

I made a face. "That wasn't my fault in there. I tripped."

"I know," she said. "But you shouldn't have yelled at him." She pulled me quickly across the street before a fast-moving cab could mow us down.

"He got what he deserved," I said, the image of the cheese on his head making me laugh.

My mom started laughing too. "It was pretty funny when that giant cheese fell on him," she agreed. That was the good thing about her—she didn't stay mad for long. I hoped she wouldn't change now that we lived in New York in rich Michael's apartment. Which reminded me. Michael had a *daughter.* I had a stepsister. I hadn't met her yet. I'd been trying to block her out of my mind, but I wouldn't be able to do that for long.

"So when is Michael's daughter coming home, anyway?" I asked.

"Tonight," my mother said. "And her name again is Mariella."

I felt my stomach sink. Mariella was thirteen and had been visiting her aunt in Switzerland for the first part of the summer. It must've been really fun—she hadn't even come to the wedding a couple of weeks before. Neither my mom nor Michael would explain why.

Michael was using the extra bedroom as an office. With the wedding and everything, he'd been too busy to switch rooms around, which meant this Mariella girl and I would have to share a bedroom until he got organized.

"You'll only be sharing the room temporarily," my mother said, as if reading my mind.

"Are you *sure* she's nice?" I asked.

"Jillian, you know I haven't met her either. I've hardly even spoken to her on the phone. But I'm sure she's lovely."

I grumbled. I couldn't get a good idea of what she might be like from her bedroom because Michael said she had taken most of her stuff to Switzerland.

My mother continued. "She's doing a lot of exciting things this summer. She even has a part-time internship as a camp counselor at the local horseback riding camp.

"Horseback riding?" I said.

"And she lost her mom a year and a half ago," my mom told me. "So she knows how hard it is, just like you."

I cocked my head. "Really?" I said thoughtfully. I didn't know anybody else whose parent had died. I wondered if Mariella got really sad about it too.

Who knew? Maybe we could be friends.

Ahead of me, several girls in ballet tights and skirts stood in a clump, laughing. One of them bought a pretzel from a street vendor and split it into three and shared the pieces with her friends. I wondered if I'd ever have friends like that in New York, girls I could share a pretzel with.

Soon enough we were in front of our new apartment building, the Dakota, on the corner of Seventy-second Street and Central Park West. It had three pointy roofs on each side, like a castle, but I thought it looked like a haunted gingerbread house.

My mom said it was a landmark or something, but I didn't care. I missed our old house, which was light and airy and had a lot of windows. I missed our yard. My dad and I liked to climb our big oak tree together.

At the Dakota's entrance, my mother looked over at the booth that stood just outside the building's large wrought iron gate. She waved to Montego, the doorman, who stood inside. He was talking on his cell phone but waved back, giving me a little wink. He pressed a button, there was a loud buzz, and the doors unlocked for us.

We walked through the courtyard, past the enormous fountain, and into the dark room where we waited for the elevator. Apparently, this crazy building had four towers and four separate elevator banks. I hadn't had time yet to explore the other towers. Our elevator was old-fashioned and dark: wood paneled—as if you were inside a coffin— with a little plush seat running along the side. What, did they think someone might need to sit down for like two seconds? Maybe a really old person, I thought. A lot of really old people lived in this building.

"I think I can smell cheese on myself," I said.

As the elevator door slid open on our floor, I could hear a series of squawking noises coming from our new apartment. I tilted my head. "What's that?" I asked.

"I don't know," my mother answered, searching for the keys. Then she looked at me excitedly. "It could be Mariella! Maybe she's back already!"

My heart started to pound.

"Why is she making that noise? Is something wrong with her?"

"Shhh," my mother said, shooting me a warning look. "Of course not. It could be her dog."

"Her *dog?*" I widened my eyes.

"Now, now," she said. "It's a small dog. A very nice dog, apparently."

"But . . . dogs are gross," I said simply. My mother raised an eyebrow.

"I'm sure he's not scary," she said. "Try to be nice."

She finally found her keys and shoved one into the lock. The door slid open, displaying our dark and gloomy foyer and incredibly prissy, can't-touch-anything living room. Sitting on a chair, looking bored and angry, was a teenage girl. She wore a sleeveless flowy dress over dark blue jeans and high-heeled sandals with skinny straps— the kind my mom would never, *ever* let me wear. The girl had long blond hair and seemed to be wearing lipstick and eyeliner. And on her lap was a tiny little animal with pointy ears and an underbite. I guessed it was a dog. I backed up a little. Michael was sitting on the couch, reading the newspaper.

The girl was talking—no, whining—into a cell phone. But when we burst into the room, she stopped talking and stared.

"Hello, Mariella," my mother began. "I'm Karen. And this is Jillian!"

"Dad," Mariella said, her cell phone still stuck to her ear, her eyes meeting mine. "Dad, she's a *baby*!"

I backed up against the wall. Mariella glared at me.

"Jillian is only two years younger than you are," Michael said, forcing a smile.

"But I'm too *old* to share a room with someone!" Mariella whined back.

"You said it would be all right when we spoke a few days ago," Michael said.

"Well, I changed my mind. Mom never would have made me share a room!"

She glared at both my mom and me and then stormed out of the room. I stared at the floor. My mom, however, had this sickly sweet smile on her face. But I noticed that her hands were trembling a little.

I raised my eyebrows at my mother. Even though Mariella's mom had died, Mariella didn't seem like she was suffering much. I didn't feel very sorry for her anymore. It felt as if there was a lump of something stuck in my throat. Maybe it was cheese.

Mrs. W and Mipsy

While we were out cheese shopping, my old bed from home had been moved into Mariella's room. Plus, Mariella had moved back in all of her personal items—a ton of clothes, jewelry, glossy magazines, posters, CDs, dog accessories, makeup, shoes. She'd stuck a whole bunch of glow-in-the-dark stars on the ceiling. I'd thought the room was pretty big before—a large square with two windows, high ceilings, and a long square mirror on one of the walls. Now my things had been shoved into the corner near the window, and the room was stuffed. I could hardly even get to my bed.

My mom was preparing for her party, so I sat in my room, staring out the window at Central Park and sketching the hot dog vendor who stood at the park's entrance.

Mariella was talking in a baby-sweet voice on her cell phone. She'd been on that thing for about three hours— she hadn't hung up since I'd gotten home. She held the phone with her shoulder, brushing her hair with one hand and petting her ratlike dog with the other. I'd overheard that the rat's name was Ramsay. My stomach knotted with despair. Mariella didn't seem all that upset about her mom. And it seemed like she'd missed her father's wedding just because she didn't feel like going.

Mariella caught me watching her and stopped her conversation. "Don't you have your own cell phone?" she snapped.

"No," I said, trying to pretend I didn't care. I went back to my sketchbook.

"God, she doesn't even have a cell phone," she muttered.

Outside our room, it sounded like the party was beginning. I heard glasses clinking together and a woman exclaiming loudly and excitedly about something called crown moldings. Mom and Michael had even hired a butler to open the door for people and take coats and bags, and caterers to serve the food.

Mariella snapped her phone closed and set it on her white dressing table, which was littered with buttons, bottles of nail polish, hair clips, ticket stubs, jewelry, dog bones, and who knows what else. She narrowed her eyes at me. "So," she said. "Jilly."

"Jilli*an*," I corrected her. Hadn't Michael told her *anything* about me?

Mariella blew her bangs upward. "Whatever. I heard you took over my room while I was in Zurich."

"I didn't take it over!" I said. "I was only here for one day!"

She eyed me carefully. "Do you get your hair done? It doesn't look like you do. It looks like you have a lot of split ends."

"I get it cut sometimes," I said.

"Well, *I* get mine blown out twice a week. *And* I get highlights. But I'm wasting my time—I'm sure you don't even know what highlights are."

"Of course I do!" I said, even though I wasn't sure. I tried to change tactics. "So, um, my mom told me about, um . . . your mom . . ."

Mariella shot me a look, then turned away.

"Well, you know that my dad—" I started.

"I don't want to talk about my mom," Mariella interrupted. "So look. Don't touch my magazines." She pointed suspiciously to the pile in the corner. "Or my jewelry. *And don't* answer my cell phone."

"Well, don't touch my sketchbook."

"Your what?" Mariella said, smirking.

I held my sketchbook close to my chest protectively. In it were drawings of all kinds of stuff—my friends from home, random faces, my feet, animals. The night before, I'd even done a couple of sketches of Michael. I'd hid behind the couch while he watched the evening news, my sketchbook propped up on my knees, studying his weathered, distinguished face and the way his salt-and-pepper hair fell across his forehead. The end result had looked pretty okay, but I felt embarrassed that I'd drawn him.

But that wasn't even the main reason I didn't want her to look—in the back of the sketchbook I'd drawn some pictures of my father. I'd copied them from old photos of him. Even though Mariella wouldn't know who he was, I didn't want her to see them.

"Whatever," Mariella said, rolling her eyes. "I wouldn't want to look at your stupid drawings. How long are you here, anyway?"

"Uh, I live here," I said.

Mariella looked pained. "The marriage won't last. That's why I didn't even go to the stupid wedding. I thought, Why bother?"

"Hey!" I said. I was right—she *didn't* care! And there I was feeling sorry for her! "That's my mom you're talking about!" I wanted to say, *Your dad's too old and boring for my mom, anyway,* but I didn't.

Just then, her horrible rat-dog Ramsay let out a bark. I jumped a little and flattened myself into the corner.

"What, are you scared of him?" Mariella laughed meanly.

"No," I said defensively.

A *tweedly-tweedly-tweedle* song interrupted us. Mariella picked up her cell phone and flipped it open.

"Hello?" she chirped, in a much nicer voice than the one she'd been using to talk to me.

I stared up at the ceiling. The door opened a crack. I looked up and saw Michael there. Mariella didn't even glance over. "Jillian," Michael said. "Just the person I was looking for. Care to join us in the living room? I have a surprise for you."

"Okay," I said cautiously. A surprise? Surprises were good, right? Maybe they were getting a divorce and I could go home!

I got off the bed and followed Michael into the crowd. A bunch of people stood around in clumps, holding long-stemmed glasses and talking. This was what my mother had made a fuss about? People standing around talking? It seemed kind of boring. Before I moved here, I thought that everyone who lived in New York City acted on Broadway or was like Donald Trump or wore really expensive, crazy outfits like the ones I'd seen on *Sex and the City* (before my mom made me change the channel), but people here looked pretty normal—we could've been in Pennsylvania. Well, except that a bunch of them wore all black, like witches.

"I want you to meet someone," Michael said. "Follow me."

I spied my mother, standing in the doorway between the living room and the dining room, wearing a sleek black dress. In her hair was a big butterfly clip I'd never seen before. It looked like it was made out of sparkly diamonds and rubies. She was really dressed up. Nothing like her usual self.

"Brie?" someone shoved a tray under my nose.

I jumped back. It smelled like Kaputsa's. And in fact, it was on a tiny purple and white striped napkin, the same pattern that was on Jacques's apron and the Kaputsa's awning. Just looking at it made me gag. I took a few steps away.

"It's imported," the person who held the tray cooed.

"No thank you," I said. "I don't like, um, imported cheese." Michael had faded into the crowd. I hoped he'd realize I wasn't behind him and come back to rescue me.

"Oh, come on, *try it!*" crowed a middle-aged woman with blunt-cut black hair and smudgy eye makeup. She wore a fur stole around her shoulders, even though it was July and a million degrees outside. Worse yet, the fur stole—I'm not even kidding—had a *face.* I stepped back from her, afraid for a second that it was alive. But it was a little dead fox face. I think it still had teeth!

The woman's hand shot out and plucked a piece of Brie off the tray. She waved it in front of my mouth. It was stinkier than stinky.

"No thanks," I said. "I don't eat cheese. I'm a, um, one of those vegetarians who don't eat anything that comes from animals."

"Silly," she said. "You need some culture! Cheese is your gateway to culture!"

And with that she popped the piece into my mouth,

like she was taking my temperature or something. It felt gooey and warm, alive—sort of like eating an earthworm. My lips puckered. I didn't know what to do. More than anything in the world I wanted to spit it out into my hand, but the woman was still staring at me.

"Isn't it *marvelous*?" she said.

"Mmm!" I mumbled. My eyes watered. I thought I might cry. Or puke.

"You children, always turning your noses up at things, but then you try them, and they're *wonderful!* Good for you for being adventurous!"

Satisfied, she patted me on the shoulder and turned away. I rushed for the bathroom sink, but the party crowd was too thick. I panicked. If I had this cheese in my mouth for much longer, I might throw up right on the expensive carpet.

Someone snickered behind me. I hoped it wasn't Mariella. When I turned, I was surprised to see an old woman in a feathery fuchsia hat, blue polka-dotted dress, and blue high-heeled shoes. She petted a tiny furry white bag. Her face was friendly and her hair was the color of lemons. If I'd had my sketchbook, I would've drawn her on the spot.

"Don't like the cheese, huh?" she said.

I shook my head.

"Here." She handed me a napkin. I was never so happy to see a napkin in my life.

"Feel better?" she asked. I nodded and stuck my tongue out to give it some air. She offered her hand. "I'm glad. I'm Mrs. Etta D. Whiteflower. I live upstairs, in the penthouse apartment."

"I'm Jillian," I said shyly, shaking her hand.

"Do you live in the building?" she asked.

I nodded a little. "I just moved here. To this apartment. And to New York."

"That's marvelous!" Mrs. Whiteflower said. "You must be Karen's daughter."

I nodded.

She smiled brightly. Her cheeks were very red. "I'm so happy to have new people in the building. I'm the head of the building events committee, you see, so I like to get to know everyone who lives here."

"So, um, you know Michael and Mariella?" I said softly.

"Yes," Mrs. Whiteflower said, and lowered her head. "Michael seems very nice. Although"—she put a finger to her lips—"between you and me and Mipsy, I'm not sure how I feel about that Mariella. But perhaps you two are best friends by now!"

"Not exactly," I said. "Who's Mispy?"

"My cat, *Mipsy.* She's my best friend. I tell her every-thing. And she tells *me* everything. There are no secrets be-tween us! Isn't that right, Mipsy? Hmmm?"

Suddenly I realized that the furry white thing in her lap wasn't a bag—it was a cat! It turned its head and looked up at me.

"I bring Mipsy with me everywhere," Mrs. W ex-plained. "Even to Central Park! I walk her on a leash! And I've taught her to walk very aristocratically."

"That's . . . great," I said. I had to admit she was pretty cute.

From behind, Michael put his hand on my shoulder. "Thought I lost you, Jillian," he said. "Oh, hello, Etta! Glad you and Mipsy could make it! I need to steal Jillian away for a moment."

Michael led me to two people wearing all black. My mother came over too.

"Robert," Michael said. The man was kind of short and had a reddish beard. "This is Jillian. My new daughter."

I cringed a little when Michael said that. Michael's hand rested calmly on my shoulder. Robert leaned down a little.

"Hello, Jillian," he said, in that obnoxious, slow voice adults use when they talk to kids.

"Hi," I said back.

"Jillian is something of an *artiste*," Michael said, making the word *artist* sound French and snobby.

"Jillian's great at drawing!" my mother chipped in. "Always drawing people!"

"Yes, she does wonderful sketches," Michael said.

I looked at Michael. When had he seen my sketches? Had he stolen my sketchbook in the middle of the night or something? Had he seen the pictures of my *father*? I started to chew on my nails.

The Robert guy rubbed his hands together like he was thinking. "I think you'd work out very well," he said.

"Work out well where?" I asked.

"You mostly draw in pencil, right?"

"Well, sometimes *colored* pencil," I said slowly. "And sometimes charcoal."

"Ahh, charcoal! A wonderful medium!"

What was going on here? Maybe I'd won a prize or something. But I hadn't entered any contest.

"Yes," I said slowly. "I have a lot of charcoal drawings, if you want to see . . ." There *was* that Design the New Post Office Mascot contest I'd entered a couple months before, but that was back in Pennsylvania. Surely this couldn't be about that—

But Michael interrupted my thoughts. "Robert runs an arts camp," he said. "You might be interested in it, Jillian. Especially if you like to draw portraits."

"Yes, it sounds *really* fun," my mom said.

"It's called Camp Powanasett," Robert continued. "It's a day camp here. We do projects all day and sketch in the park sometimes. Lots of interesting kids attend. There are other outdoor activities too. Sports and things. You like sports?"

"I don't know," I said. From Michael's and my mother's eager looks, it seemed like my answer should be yes. I couldn't bear to look at their expectant faces.

"So does that sound fun?" my mother asked with a gigantic smile.

"I guess," I said slowly, trying to be polite.

"Great!" my mom said. "I'm so glad you're excited. Because I wanted it to be a surprise, for tonight—we've already signed you up!"

"Oh," I said weakly.

My mom gave Robert a nod.

I tried to keep the tears from coming. I was going to this camp whether I liked it or not. I had planned on spending the summer lying around the house, watching TV, drawing, and feeling a little sorry for myself, not at some stupid camp!

"You'll love the camp," Robert said, turning to me again. "The bus picks you up tomorrow. Right in front of the Dakota."

"*Tomorrow!*" I squeaked, my mouth dropping open. "I don't . . . I'm not . . ."

But it was too late. They were all talking to each other now. This was going to be the worst summer ever.

Rainbow

The thing that I realized pretty quickly about New York City in the summer was that it smelled really, really bad. The next morning, as my mother and I waited down on the corner of Seventy-second Street and Central Park West for the camp bus, all the smells floated right up to my nose. Beneath me, I felt the rumblings of the subway. I was never going to get used to it here.

I couldn't believe I was going to camp. I hadn't gotten any sleep. The party had gone on until really late. But even after it ended, I still couldn't sleep because Mariella stayed on her stupid cell phone half the night. And she actually was trying to be quiet, but I could hear everything—she was talking on and on about some boy she liked.

"He told Amelia he wanted to take me to Ruby Foo's," she'd whispered into the phone. "And then Kate told me he asked about me the other day at the Reservoir, but Jenny? She's at Juilliard for the summer, and *she* said she saw him getting off the one-nine at Sixty-sixth *with another girl*! And they got pretzels from the hot dog cart!"

"Please let me sleep!" I'd finally bellowed at about three in the morning. But she didn't. Whoever the boy was, he sounded like a creep. Probably picked his nose.

So now there I stood in front of the Dakota, getting ready for a day at stupid Camp Somethingorother. "It's going to be so much fun!" my mother said, squeezing my hand. "You're lucky Michael pulled some strings. There's often a waiting list."

A cheery-looking yellow bus slid up to the curb. It was covered with really badly painted kid faces, scribbly clouds, triangular trees, and a large block-lettered CAMP POW-WOW emblazoned on the side.

The door slid open, and a scruffy older bus driver peered down at me. "Good morning!" he said, beaming brightly. "What's your name?"

"Jillian Fairley," I muttered.

"She's new," my mother added.

He looked at his clipboard. "Aha!" he said. "There you are! Welcome! My name is Fred! Climb aboard!"

He was way too happy for eight o'clock in the morning. I climbed onto the bus, waving halfheartedly to my mom. Then I turned back to check out the other kids.

Yikes. Sitting at the front were a bunch of terrified little kids, six-year-olds, maybe, clutching paper-bag lunches. One girl sucked crazily at her thumb. At the back sat two rows of teenagers. Mostly boys. They all wore oversized sweatshirts—even though it was a million degrees outside—and scowls. One large boy in an extra-large bright orange polo shirt had a boom box turned up to maximum volume. Loud music was coming out of the speakers; it sounded like Snoop Dogg. I wondered who had made these guys sign up for art camp.

Great. I sat in an empty seat in the middle and clunked my head against the window.

"So, Jillian," the bus driver called from up front. "Do you like Snoop Dogg?"

"*What?*" I said. I'd never heard an old person say *Snoop Dogg.*

"The music. Isn't that Snoop Dogg? How about singing me some lyrics!"

"Um . . . ," I said. Was he kidding? I stared out the window and pretended I didn't hear him.

We pulled up to a sign that said Barnard College, drove through a wrought iron gate, and stopped at a brick building. The bus door swung open, and the kids began to pile out. I stepped out too, and looked around. Wait. I thought we were going to Camp Pow-Wow-Something. But we were still in Manhattan, I was sure of it. And it looked like we were going into a school!

"See ya later!" the bus driver said happily as I got out.

A young woman in a long flowy skirt and clunky sandals walked up to me. She had a flower painted on her cheek, a silver nose ring, and about twenty braids in her hair.

"Are you Jillian?" she asked, blinking quickly a bunch of times, as if she had something stuck in her eye.

I nodded.

"I'm Rainbow!" she said. "I'm your counselor!"

"Rainbow?" I said.

"Well, it's actually Rebecca," she said, adjusting her silvery bangle bracelets. "But I'm much more in *touch* with the name Rainbow!"

"Okay," I said, feeling a little shaky. I hoped she wouldn't ask me to change *my* name. I followed her into the building and down a long hallway and noticed that the backs of her legs were super sunburned and covered in bug bites.

"Camp Powanasett is for kids with all kinds of interests," Rainbow said as we walked. "I'm the counselor for the visual arts kids. We're going to do lots of stuff that's important to the growing artist!"

She led me into a fluorescent-lit classroom.

"Okay, everyone, gather around!" Rebecca—er, Rainbow—said, clapping her hands. "Everyone come into the peace circle!" She reached behind the desk and pulled out a bongo.

The other kids, who had been sitting at desks, obediently got up and sat in a circle on the grimy linoleum floor. I was the only one standing. Rainbow gently gestured that I should sit. Reluctantly, I did. The floor was a little sticky.

"Okay, everyone," Rainbow said. "We are now in the peace circle. Do we all feel peaceful?"

"Yes," the other kids murmured.

Not really, I thought.

Rainbow continued. "Today we're going to get in touch with our inner artists." She started playing the bongo slowly. Then she closed her eyes and began to hum. "Close your eyes and join hands!" she ordered. "We are a circle of artists!"

What in the world was this? I looked to the kids on my right and left. Their eyes were closed, and their hands were flexing for me to grab them. The boy next to me had a hand that was way too grubby and smudgy to hold. I clasped his thumb, which seemed the cleanest. And the girl on my other side had a hand that was colder than a glacier.

"MmmmmmmmmMMMMmmm," Rainbow began to hum as she continued to beat on the bongo.

"MMMmmmm," the others echoed. I didn't hum along.

"Now, artists, everyone call out your own special sound!" Rainbow said, speeding up her drumbeats. "Think about how you feel about art today, and express it to the class! My sound is CHEEEEEEeee! Everyone say it: CHEEEeee!"

My eyes sprang open. She sounded like a crazed monkey. This *had* to be a joke. But then the kids all echoed her. And worse, she started calling out kids' names so that they could express their *own* sounds. "Brian!" she shouted. And the dirty-fingered boy next to me bellowed, "Mooooooowww." Like a sick cow. Everyone, their eyes still closed, imitated him.

She continued around the circle. Kids called out weird sounds. My heart beat fast. I didn't even like giving book reports in front of my class. This was *definitely* not for me.

But Rainbow didn't know that. And so, eventually, drumming frantically, she called, "Jillian!"

I didn't have a sound. Everyone waited. The drum thumped. "Uh, I'd rather . . . not," I murmured.

"What's that?" Rainbow said.

"I'd rather not!" I said more loudly.

"Everyone!" Rainbow called.

And then everyone imitated me: "I'd rather not," they all said, in voices that sounded weirdly like mine.

"No!" I shouted. "That's not what I meant—"

Too late. Rainbow's bongo drowned me out and she moved on to the next kid.

This went on for maybe another half hour. We went through more sounds, and then singing, and then everyone took turns with the bongo. No one was shy except me. I felt humiliated and worn out. Finally, we broke for lunch. Hopefully we'd get to do some drawing after that. We were certainly spiritually prepared for it.

But to my horror, after lunch Rainbow clapped her hands and said, "All right, everyone! It's time for field day!"

Everyone except me cheered.

I had nothing against exercise. I liked to swim and stuff. But I certainly didn't like the sound of something called *field day*. I thought this was supposed to be an arts camp!

Rainbow herded us out into the hall and gathered all the other, nonvisual arts kids, which included the thugs from the back of my bus. "Where are we going?" I asked a girl next to me, whose special sound in the peace circle had been "googlygooglygoo."

"Central Park," she lisped.

"Are we *walking*?" I said, in a voice that sounded a little like Mariella's.

"It's only a couple of blocks," the girl said, moving away from me as if I had chicken pox.

It had to be a hundred degrees out. The garbage-day smell wafted into my nostrils. Rainbow and the other counselors lined us up with partners and led us out of Barnard's gates. We walked two by two over to the park. After what seemed like an hour of walking, we got to a brown patchy strip of land in Central Park. I looked around me. Three quarters of the kids wore neon-colored CAMP POWANASETT T-shirts. The others wore heavy sweatshirts. Weren't they *dying*? The counselors had brought out a large gym bag, which they turned upside down in the middle of the dirt field, revealing about a hundred burlap sacks.

"Come on, Jillian!" Rainbow cried, shoving me toward the field. "Get a good sack!"

I looked back and forth. The other campers were frantically running for the pile of sacks as if they were going to get free ice cream or something. By the time I wove through them, there was only one sack left in the dirt. It had a giant hole in it.

"It's okay!" Rainbow cooed when she saw me stick my finger through the sack's hole. "That means it's a *special sack*! It's had a lot of love! Now, come on!" She nudged me to the starting line. "Get hopping!"

Swallowing hard, I lined up with the others to start the race. The counselor blew the whistle and everyone started hopping. Except me. My foot immediately went through the hole, and I sprawled onto the ground—right into a puddle. A bunch of kids bounced right over me, a few of them stepping on my legs and arms. "Ow!" I squealed.

"Goooooooo, Jillian!" Rainbow cheered from the sidelines. "Get up, get up!"

I had to get out of there.

Somehow I managed to cross the finish line before some dinky six-year-olds. As soon as I did, I wriggled out of my sack and ducked behind a tree. I had to think of a plan.

There was a large cluster of trees ahead. If I could get to them, maybe I could slink away. I had seen the street signs when we walked from Barnard to the park and knew that we were heading downtown. Maybe I could walk home! I had keys, and Montego would let me into the building.

At the finish line, one of the six-year-olds had fallen into the dust, and then another six-year-old tripped over her, and then another, and suddenly it became this seven-kid pile-up in the middle of the field. All the counselors rushed over, trying to untangle the kids from the sacks. No one was watching me. I made a dash for the trees.

I crouched behind a big oak.

"Jillian?" I heard Rainbow call. "Where's Jillian?"

"I thought I saw her over there," said a little kid, pointing in my direction. I looked behind me. I saw a little asphalt path through the trees.

"Jillian!" I heard Rainbow call. Uh-oh, I thought, my heart beating like mad. I had to move fast.

Central Park West was shady and calm. I was so happy to be away from camp, I was actually sort of enjoying the walk.

"Jillian?"

I looked up, expecting to see Rainbow. But there, in front of me, was my mom.

Uh-oh.

She looked really mad. "What are you doing?" she said, hands on her hips. "Why aren't you at camp?"

"I . . . ," I squeaked. What was she doing in this neighborhood at this time of day? I thought her office was somewhere on Fifty-second Street!

"Well?" she said, looking madder and madder by the second.

"Umm . . . ," I said. "Well, we're back there in the park . . ."

She sighed. "Come on. I don't want you running around the city by yourself. We have to get you back to the counselors."

"They aren't expecting me back!" I said desperately.

But my mom saw right through that. She grabbed me by the arm and led me back into the park. I hung my head.

We were silent for a while, and I was a little afraid my mom was going to kill me or something. But finally, she broke the silence.

"I know this is hard," she said. "Moving here, making all these changes, being away from your friends. It's hard for me, too."

"Hmm," I said.

"It is!" my mother said. "I've uprooted my life as well, honey. But we have to make the best of it."

"I want to go home," I said. Then I added, in my head, *Dad would never have made me go to camp.* But it was too mean, so I didn't say it out loud.

"Oh, Jillian," my mom sighed. She stopped and faced me. "*Please* give New York and camp a chance," she said. "If you don't go to camp, I'll have to get you a babysitter for the summer."

"A babysitter!" I squealed. I hadn't had a babysitter in a year.

"Yes," my mother said, folding her arms across her chest. "Oh, and another thing, please try to be nicer to Mariella. She said you were very unfriendly toward her last night."

"*What?!?*" I shrieked. "*Mariella* said that? To *you*?"

My mother nodded. "Yes, she said it this morning, after you left."

"*She's* the one who's unfriendly!" I said, my voice rising higher and higher by the minute. "She's . . . she's *mean*! She *hates* me, Mom!"

"Jillian! Of course she doesn't," my mom said.

"She said she didn't even come to the wedding because she couldn't be bothered!" I yelled. There. That'd change my mom's mind.

But my mother just kept walking.

We approached the field again. Now the campers were doing some relay race that involved a spongy ball and weird plastic tubing. "That looks fun," my mother said.

I grunted.

"Jilly!" Rainbow wailed, rushing up to me. "Oh my goodness, I thought you were dead! We sent Bart, the musicians' counselor, over to the Sheep Meadow to look for you because we thought maybe you wandered over there, and we sent some people to the Reservoir . . ." She looked as if she was about to cry. "I'm just so happy you're all right!" She waved her arms up and down and all her silvery bracelets clanged together.

"I was just—" I started.

"I'm Jillian's mom," my mother said to Rainbow. "I found her on Central Park West. I'm sorry for all the trouble she's caused." She gave me a stern look before walking away.

"We'll have to keep an eye on you, Jilly!" Rainbow said in her old cheery voice. "Hmm, I should alert the search party that you've been found. Perhaps I can do it telepathically." She put her fingers to her temples. "Ommmm," she hummed. "Come in, Jordan. Jilly has been found. . . ."

"It's Jill*ian*," I said, but Rainbow didn't hear me.

MIPSY
...the most wonderful
kitty in the world!

After my first day of camp, I sat in the Dakota's elevator with my sketchbook on my lap and rode up and down, watching as people got in and out. As soon as they stepped out, I'd quickly draw a picture of them. I was racking up some pretty neat sketches—some of them were cartoony and others were serious. It was way better than hanging out in the apartment thinking about my horrible day. So I went up and down, up and down. Until, on my seventh ride of the hour, the doors slid open on the penthouse floor and a familiar-looking cat sped into the elevator.

"Whoa," I said.

As the elevator doors closed, I heard a voice scream, "My Mipsy!" It was that woman from the party, Mrs. Whiteflower. I pressed the Door Open button, but it was too late. I could hear Mrs. Whiteflower screaming through the heavy oak doors, "Cat on the loose! My poor Mipsy!"

Mipsy seemed pretty freaked out too. She squashed herself up into the corner of the elevator.

"It's okay, kitty," I cooed to her. She looked up at me with the cutest blue eyes and started to purr.

Before the doors could slide open in the lobby, I hit the button for the penthouse floor again. I heard someone outside the elevator say, "Hey!"—most likely angry that I had left without them. But I couldn't worry about that now. I needed to return Mipsy to Mrs. W right away.

The doors opened again at the penthouse, and there was a worried-looking Mrs. W.

She wore glasses with electric-blue frames and her hair was piled up on top of her head in a tall bun. Hanging from her ears were dangly earrings shaped like lightbulbs. Her nails were painted purple. As soon as she saw Mipsy and me, she let out a wail.

"Mipsy! I thought I'd lost you!"

She dove for the cat and scooped her up. "My Mipsy-Wipsy, I'm sorry we got into a fight! Oh, goodness, I'm so glad you're back!" She was even making kissy noises.

Finally Mrs. W turned to me. "Jillian!" she said. I was

surprised she remembered my name. "Oh, thank you thank you thank you! I thought my Mipsy was lost forever!"

"I guess she wanted to ride on the elevator," I said, walking over to the cat and tickling her under the chin.

Mrs. W held Mipsy tightly to her chest. "How can I thank you? Would you like a soda or something?"

"Okay," I said. "She sure is cute." I petted Mipsy's head.

"You like animals?" Mrs. W asked.

"I like cats," I said. "But not dogs." I made a face.

"Yes, cats are much better than dogs," Mrs. W said. "Especially Mipsy. Did you ever have a cat of your own?"

"No," I said. "But back in Pennsylvania, my next-door neighbors, the Hernandezes, had this super-fat cat, Big D, who spent a lot of time at my house. Sometimes we'd leave food out on our porch for Big D, and she'd come over and eat it. When the Hernandezes went away I'd cat-sit, so I got to know Big D pretty well. I really loved her."

All of a sudden Mrs. W looked up at me with a big smile on her face.

"I just had an idea," she said, very dramatically. Then she started jumping up and down like a little kid, taking Mipsy along with her. "Oh yes, this is a splendid idea!"

"What?" I said, hoping she wasn't having some kind of crazy old lady fit.

"Well, you see, I was offered a residency at an artists' colony in Maine, to do my sculpture. But they don't allow cats. And my cat-sitter just canceled, so I'd decided that I couldn't go."

"That's too bad," I said.

She looked at me. "*You* wouldn't want to watch her for me, would you? I could give you keys, and you could play with her and feed her, and, oh, it would be easy! I'll pay you, of course. I'll pay you . . . let's say . . . twenty-five dollars a day."

"A *day*?" I said. "Are you serious?"

"Yes, is that too little? I don't know what children make these days." As if most kids worked steady jobs.

"No, twenty-five dollars is great," I said. "Watching Mipsy sounds like fun."

"Well, that's wonderful! That means I can do my residency after all!" Mrs. W said. She shoved her key into the lock. "We will, of course, need to get permission from your mother, too. I'll call her tonight!"

"Okay," I said, though I wasn't sure my mother would say yes after that afternoon.

I walked into Mrs. W's apartment. It was super, super cool. The walls were all painted in different colors—red, orange, sea-foam green. There were interesting wire towers, wild wire animals, and, hanging from the ceiling, intricate, cartoonish wire airplanes. On the walls were giant colorful paintings, mostly of people. The kind of stuff I'd like to paint someday. The furniture was cool too: funky without being stuffy, like ours was. I ran my hands along a purple velvet sofa, a leopard-spotted chair, a funny, irregular-shaped bookshelf, a wire-sculpture Eiffel Tower on the glass coffee table. On one living room wall hung a big portrait of someone's lips. A big flat-screen TV hung on the opposite wall. Stacks of DVDs and books were splayed out all over the coffee table. There was even a Sunkist soda machine humming away in the corner.

"Wow. Your apartment is so cool," I said. "I love those wire sculptures."

"Oh yes, those old things," she said. "I made those, actually."

"Wow," I said. "And the Sunkist machine works?" Sunkist was my favorite kind of soda.

"Yep. No change required. I'm a little addicted to sugary beverages." Mrs. W. winked. "Help yourself."

Strawberry Sunkist in my hand, I peeked into the bathroom and saw an enormous tub. "Whoa," I said. Mrs. W had all kinds of funny rubber toys lined up along the tub's rim. There was a duck with devil's horns, a rubber giraffe in an inner tube, and a porcupine with sunglasses. Back out in the main room, I saw a whole bunch of Winsor & Newton paint sets on one of the lower bookshelves. I counted three acrylic sets, two oils, a watercolor, and even pastels.

"There is paper in this filing drawer here," Mrs. W said behind me, pulling out a drawer to reveal sheets and sheets of high-quality artists' paper. "And empty canvases in the other room. I even have a potter's wheel in the office over there."

"This is amazing," I said. I'd hit the jackpot.

"You can use anything you'd like while I'm gone," Mrs. W said, smiling. "You'll have so much fun!"

"Wow," I said, overwhelmed. I wondered if Mrs. W was really serious—if she'd pay me twenty-five dollars a day *and* let me use all her art stuff. What would I do with twenty-five dollars a day? I could buy a bus ticket out of this city, for one thing. Back to Pennsylvania.

"Now," Mrs. W said. "Here is where I keep Mipsy's water and food, and over there are her scratching toys." She showed me how to change the litter and where Mipsy's favorite treats were, and told me what games she liked to play. She picked up some toy mice, and Mipsy got really excited and began to dance around.

"C'mon Mips, go get the mouse!" I said, picking some up and tossing them down the long corridor.

Mipsy, tail in the air, skidded to chase them. She stuffed two or three mice in her mouth and pranced proudly back to me, purring loudly. She looked so cute and funny, I couldn't help falling in love with her.

"Here is an extra set of keys," Mrs. W said, handing me a small key ring. "Now, don't go using these keys for other people's apartments!" She giggled.

"What do you mean?" I asked.

"Oh, it's an old joke. The builders in this neighborhood used to install the same locks in every door, to save money. Goodness, I have to pack!" She fluttered about the room.

"So these keys might open *my* apartment?" I asked curiously.

"Perhaps! I once needed to get inside a friend's apartment—she lived on Seventy-eighth Street—and I tried my keys in her locks, and lo and behold, they worked!"

"That's crazy," I said, looking carefully at the keys. "That doesn't sound very safe."

Mrs. W shrugged. "Well, not that many people know

about it. The only other thing I ask of you is that you call me at the residency number every day—I'll leave it on the refrigerator—and let me talk to Mipsy. We have a very close relationship, and she might feel very hurt if we don't speak every day. You see, she doesn't know how to use the telephone herself. Silly girl."

"Oh, yes," I said, as if some cats actually did know how to use the telephone. "Well, I can do that. No problem."

"Very good! So it's settled. Now I need to relax." She went over to the Sunkist machine and got herself a soda. She opened the can, sat down on her purple sofa, and put her feet up. "Ahhhh," she said, gazing out the window. Hers was a different view than I had—she looked out onto Seventy-second Street instead of Central Park West. And her apartment was higher up than mine. It was the penthouse, which meant it was the only apartment on the top floor.

"I could look out the window all day," she said finally.

"I look out the window and draw people," I said. Mipsy's silky body wound around me, and I scratched her ears.

"So you're serious about art? Have you been to the museums yet?"

"Not yet," I said.

"Oh, but you must!" Mrs. W said. "They're some of the most wonderful things about New York!"

"Yeah, New York," I said uncertainly.

"What," Mrs. W said, "you don't like it here?"

I frowned. "Not yet."

"But it's the most wonderful city in the world!" Mrs. W whooped.

"I just feel wrong here," I said. "And shy. And I miss home. I really, really miss home." *And my dad,* I thought. But I didn't add that.

Mrs. W narrowed her eyes at me. "You are an artist, my dear. New York *is* your home. You might not realize it now, but you will soon. And it will inspire you. Believe me." She took another long sip of her Sunkist, and I did the same.

"Okay," I said, still unsure. I hoped she was right, but what Mrs. W said didn't sound too convincing. But hey, I was going to be making twenty-five dollars a day. With that I could get away from Mariella, away from the peace circle, away from the stinky, sweaty, New York City streets, and never see any of it again.

trademark
feather
boa

riding
hat

Emily
...lives in the building!

6

After about a week, my days had started to take on a pattern. Wake up at seven-thirty, glare at Mariella as she caked on her makeup at her dressing table. Agonize at breakfast as my mom said things to Mariella like "I made some cinnamon swirl toast *especially* for you, Mariella!" and "Oh, Mariella, your camp-counselor-in-training job sounds like so much fun! Why don't you tell us about it?"

Then I was out on the sidewalk, inhaling the stink (I swear I needed one of those weird gas masks I saw an action hero wear in a movie once), and on the bouncing, Snoop Dogg–thumping bus at eight-thirty. My mom stopped coming down with me to wait once she was satisfied that I wasn't going to run off again. I was tempted, but I remembered my mom's threat: if she caught me again, she'd have to get me a babysitter. And I was too old for a babysitter. Mariella would have *way* too much fun teasing me about *that*.

One morning, I was waiting for the bus when I caught sight of a familiar-looking man. It wasn't until he was up close that I realized who it was: that scary cheese man from Kaputsa's. He was barreling up Central Park West, cradling a giant wheel of cheese in his arms! Quickly, I looked down. I didn't think he noticed me; he muttered in French as he walked by, the key around his neck thumping against his chest, and he nearly crashed into a street sign.

Camp was generally one horrible day after the next. The bus driver kept trying to talk to me. He probably felt sorry for me because I didn't have anyone else to talk to on the bus. And at camp we hardly got to draw, but instead did a lot of Rainbow's "artist exercises," which meant a lot of chanting and drumming in the Peace Circle. Once, we spent half the morning sitting cross-legged on the floor, breathing very deeply and not saying a word. Rainbow instructed us to find our "inner third eye." Half the kids tipped over, curled up on the sticky school floor, and fell asleep. The only time we actually did any artwork was when Rainbow gave us poster paints and ordered us to paint all over one another's faces. My partner was the boy with the smudgy hands, and I was *not* happy touching his face, even if I did get to slap poster paint all over it.

Every afternoon, we trudged over to the park. The sun seemed to get hotter and hotter as the days went on.

Then I'd get home to the wonderful air-conditioning of Mrs. W's place. At least my mom had said that I could watch Mipsy while Mrs. W was away. I'd play hide-and-seek with Mipsy and serve her kitty treats on a silver platter I found in Mrs. W's cupboard. I painted her portrait with acrylic paints and took a bubble bath in the giant tub, dumping all the funny rubber animals into the water with me.

I looked through Mrs. W's closets, too. She had a ton of outfits—many of which, she said, had been custom made for her by famous or up-and-coming designers. I sifted through hanger after hanger of tulle and satin and lace gowns, each smelling slightly moldy. Still, they weren't the typical poufy dresses that girls wear to the prom or to some stupid homecoming dance. These dresses were works of art. Some had feathers all over them. One was covered by a large sequined butterfly. Another was a collage of strange objects—parts looked like metal, and I noticed a cut up credit card sewn into a sleeve. She had crazy-looking hats, too—sun hats with giant brims, a huge collection of 1920s-style flapper hats, and even a ritzy-looking Santa hat, complete with a ball of mink fluff on the end. I wondered where she'd worn that.

There was one hat, made of millions of tiny white feathers and beads, that looked a little like a fancy coconut cake. I liked that one the best. It came in a cool silvery heart-shaped hatbox. When I put it on my head and looked in the mirror, I didn't recognize myself. I looked mysterious. I found a pair of big sunglasses on Mrs. W's dresser. I put them on too. I looked older. Maybe thirteen or fourteen. I definitely *didn't* look like I'd been chanting in a peace circle all day.

I tried on most of Mrs. W's dresses, but every day I went back to that hat and sunglasses combination. I balanced my sketchbook next to the mirror and drew pictures of myself wearing it. They came out pretty good.

After I was done at Mrs. W's, I'd usually go down to the lobby to talk to Montego the doorman. We'd sort of become friends. Montego was young and used nice-smelling hair gel. I liked his Spanish accent, and he always told me really silly jokes. ("Why did the monkey fall out of the tree?" was one. The answer: "'Cause he was dead." I thought it was pretty funny.) I liked to stand in the little booth with him, and sometimes he gave me bites of his Cuban sandwiches, which were made of ham and cheese (but good, *unstinky* cheese) on warm, fresh bread. He knew everybody in the building—*and* knew everything about them. Including Mariella.

"Once," he said in his Spanish accent, "she came out here to get a cab, and got really mad when I couldn't get one for her, and had a temper tantrum! Said she was going to call up her daddy and *then* I'd be sorry!"

"Wow," I said. "That's awful, but it does sound like her."

"But, you know, I recently saw Mariella down here, right along that wall right there, crying her eyes out."

Mariella, crying? "It was probably about some boy or something," I said.

Montego gave me a dubious look. "I don't know," he said. "I don't think so."

Huh.

I walked through the lobby, thinking about what Montego had said about Mariella. Then *oof!*

I crashed right into a girl in front of me. She was wearing tall riding boots and carrying a heavy-looking helmet.

"Watch where you're going!" the girl shouted.

"*Sorry,*" I said. This was probably some crony of Mariella's. Her T-shirt was from the horseback-riding camp Mariella worked at. But then she turned around, and I recognized her.

"Is it . . . Emily?" I asked.

"Yes! Jill . . . Jillian?" she answered.

It was the girl with the Pumas and the boa that I had met in Kaputsa's cheese department.

"What are you doing here?" I asked.

"I live here!" she said.

"You *do?*" I said. "I do too! But . . . I've never *seen* you . . ."

"Yeah, I live in five-D," Emily said. "It's the west elevator bank." My apartment was on the east bank. "But you probably haven't seen me because I've been at camp." She made a face.

"It can't be worse than *my* camp," I said.

"Where are you?"

"Camp Powanasett."

"Ohmygod! My parents made me go there one year! Did they make you do sack racing yet?"

"*Yes*," I said. "It was terrible. I tried to escape!"

"I'm at a riding camp this summer," Emily explained. "All I do, all day, is ride horses. Or brush horses. Or clean up horse poop. You know what's really funny, though?" she asked, switching her helmet from one hand to the other. "I *hate horses!*"

With that, we both burst into giggles.

"I don't like being that high up on anything," Emily said. "And . . . horses smell! I'd much rather be at this acting camp in the Village. I want to be an actress, you know. But my mother wouldn't let me." She made a face. "She said I should learn to ride horses, for some dumb reason."

"My evil stepsister is working at your camp," I said. "Mariella?"

"Really? She's your stepsister?" Emily said.

"Yep."

"She's a snob," Emily said. "She won't talk to me even though she knows we live in the same building!"

"Well, she's snobby to me and we live in the same apartment!" I said.

We sat down by the fountain in the inner courtyard. "Have you been back to Kaputsa's?" Emily asked.

"No," I said. "But I accidentally had a taste of the really stinky cheese!"

"Gross!" Emily said.

"I gagged," I said, making a face. "I couldn't get the taste out of my mouth for *days.*"

I'd never sat by the Dakota's fountain before. It was really nice. You could see different wings of the Dakota—

they were like little turrets on a big castle—and I could even see my own apartment. I could see the back of Mrs. W's, too, way up at the top. I told Emily I was cat-sitting for Mrs. W. She sounded excited. I could already tell we'd be friends.

"Are you busy now?" I asked. "Do you want to come hang out and play with Mipsy?"

"Sure, I love Mrs. Whiteflower," Emily said happily. "She always organizes the Dakota Christmas parties. And you know what? Last time, she organized a Christmas *pageant*! And everyone in the building had to be in it! She *forced* everyone!"

"Really?" I said. "That's crazy!"

"All these stuffy businessmen had to be elves," Emily went on. "And there was this famous actress who lives here who had to play a reindeer!"

"That sort of sounds like the stuff I have to do at camp," I said. "This counselor I have, her name's Rainbow, and—"

"Oh, no!" Emily interrupted. "Jillian, I *remember* Rainbow. What a super freak!"

We stepped into the elevator. "I can't wait to see Mrs. W's apartment," Emily said.

"It's really cool. *And* it's a great place for me to get away from Mariella."

"You know the thing that's weird about Mariella?" Emily asked. "Most of the time she's totally mean, but lately, she just kind of mopes around, frowning."

"Probably about a boy," I said. "She won't stop talking on the phone about some boy she likes. He probably doesn't even know she exists. . . ."

Just then, the elevator doors lurched open. I thought it was Mrs. W's floor and made a motion to get out.

But to my surprise, it was my floor. And there before us was Mariella, standing in front of the hall mirror, checking out her butt. She was so absorbed in her reflection, she didn't see Emily or me. She had her hands cradled around her butt and had even pulled up her shorts a little to get a look at the backs of her legs, which were pasty white and slightly hairy.

Emily snorted. Mariella quickly turned away from the mirror. Her eyes narrowed at me. But we'd seen everything. Her face was beet red. And, thank goodness, the doors closed before she could say anything!

Safe with the elevator doors closed, Emily and I looked at each other and collapsed into giggles.

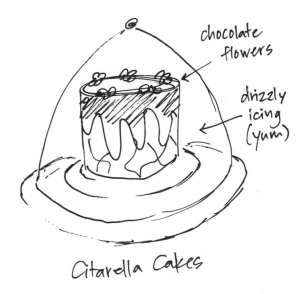

chocolate
flowers

drizzly
icing
(yum)

Citarella Cakes

7

"This place is awesome!" Emily cried, looking around Mrs. W's apartment.

Emily wandered through the apartment while I refilled Mipsy's water and food dishes. Then, from the kitchen, she screamed. "Jillian! Have you *seen this*?"

"What?" I screamed back, running into Mrs. W's shiny, state-of-the art kitchen.

"*Look,*" Emily said, pointing through a door into what I had thought was a broom closet. But inside the alcove, there was a second fridge. I was afraid Emily was pointing at something horrible, like a dead rat or maybe a giant wheel of Brie. But inside the refrigerator were cakes.

That's right. Cakes. All different kinds. A chocolate-iced one, a white-iced one, a carrot cake, a Black Forest cake. Cakes with gooey icing, delicate sugary flower work, drizzled chocolate and white chocolate–dipped strawberries around the edges. I smelled chocolate and bananas and sugar. My mouth watered. They were all under fancy glass domes. Not a bite had been taken out of any of them.

"What do you think these are *for*?" Emily whispered.

One of the domes had a note taped to it. JILLIAN, it read in large, spiky letters. Next to it was a picture of the bird sculpture that hung in the foyer.

I grabbed the note and opened it. *Dear Jillian, Thought you might enjoy some Citarella cakes. Thank you again for watching my precious Mipsy.*

"These are for me!" I gasped, my eyes boggling. Each cake looked more delicious than the last.

"Well, then, which one should we eat first?" Emily asked, pirouetting around the room, looking for the silverware drawer.

I smiled. Mariella wouldn't have gone anywhere near these cakes, claiming she was on some kind of diet and that just *looking* at the cakes would make her fat. Emily was my kind of girl.

We pulled all the cakes out of the fridge and arranged them on the large oak kitchen table. "They look too beautiful to eat," I whispered reverently.

"Let's try the prettiest one first," Emily said.

"That's definitely the coconut cake," I said. "I'll get a knife."

We cut into it. Chocolate oozed out. "Oh, yummy," Emily said excitedly.

"Let's cut a bunch of slices and bring them into the other room," I said. I opened cabinets to look for plates. "Here we go," I said, bringing down two giant serving platters. "These should be big enough."

We cut pieces of the coconut cake, the chocolate mocha cake, the coffee swirl cake, the white chocolate–dipped strawberry shortcake, and the Black Forest cake. We started eating, smacking our lips and making appreciative oohs and aahs.

"We need music," I said. "Mrs. W has a ton of CDs."

"Does she have any show tunes?" Emily asked.

We looked: Mrs. W had a really big collection of old show tunes. "I love *The Sound of Music*!" Emily squealed, clutching a CD. "Let's put it on!"

Emily began dancing around the room, singing, "The hills are alive . . . with the sound of music!" Then, tired of spinning, she flung herself down on the couch.

"You have a great voice," I said.

"Thanks! I want to be on Broadway someday," she said.

For a while, the only sounds in the apartment were the *Sound of Music* CD and our forks clinking against the plates. Then Emily burst into giggles.

"Look at Mipsy," she said. "She's driving her scratching car!"

I burst out laughing. Sure enough, Mrs. W's cat was in the driver's seat of the scratching Mercedes. Emily leapt up from her plate and, making motor noises, began to push Mipsy around. Mipsy meowed, as if this was the most fun she'd ever had.

"This is so, so good," Emily gushed, sitting down again. "I could keep eating . . . until I popped!"

Then, struck with an idea, Emily laid down her fork. "Did you say Mrs. W had outfits and stuff?"

"Tons! Let me show you!"

We dove into Mrs. W's closets. Emily's jaw dropped as she sifted through the sparkly, gauzy gowns. "These are beautiful," she whispered. She pulled out a robin's egg blue dress and a short pink and black one.

"I've tried that one on," I said, pointing to the pink and black one. "It's really cool."

"I wonder where Mrs. W wears all these dresses?" Emily said. "Maybe she goes to royal balls!"

She pulled out a sea-foam green dress with an elaborate swirl of fabric at the bottom. "Here, try this on," she said. I slid on the green dress. It was way too long on me.

"You look like a mermaid!" Emily snorted with laughter.

Emily dug farther in Mrs. W's closet and pulled out big bulky motorcycle boots with HARLEY-DAVIDSON MOTOR-CYCLES inscribed on the sides.

"Whoa, I can't see Mrs. W wearing those!" I said. Emily slid them onto her feet. They were enormous and clunky; she looked really silly.

I tried on the coconut cake hat and big sunglasses for her. "What do you think?" I said. "Do I look older?"

"Definitely," Emily said. "That hat is really cool. And I don't even recognize you!"

Our sugar high dropping fast, we both curled up on the couch and put in a DVD of *Breakfast at Tiffany's*. I stole away for a few minutes to call Mrs. W and thank her for the cakes. Then, when Mrs. W asked to speak to Mipsy in private, I put the phone down for Mipsy and wandered back into the TV room. Restless, I opened up another drawer in Mrs. W's living room. Inside were a whole bunch of photographs and a large pair of binoculars. I pulled out the photographs and realized that they were of some people that I recognized from the elevators. The tall guy who always wore the crisp suits and hats. The hand-holding couple. The businessman who looked and acted like the White Rabbit from *Alice in Wonderland*, always looking at his watch.

"What do you think these are?" I asked Emily, taking the drawer to her. There must have been hundreds of photographs inside.

"These are from the Christmas party I told you about!" Emily said. "Mrs. W organizes it. All the people in the building come. This was from last year. See? There's Mrs. W in a Santa hat."

I flipped through some more and, to my surprise, came upon one of Michael. He was dressed in a suit. His eyes looked drawn and his mouth tired. He stood underneath a giant chandelier.

"Where is this room?" I said, pointing to the chandelier.

"Oh, this party wasn't here," Emily explained. "It was for the Dakota tenants, but the courtyard was being repaired last year, so we had to have it in the ballroom of the apartment building across the street."

"Oh," I said, flipping to the next picture. Another one of Michael. And standing next to him was a very bratty-looking Mariella. Her mouth was turned down in a pout, and her eyes were rolled in exasperation up to the sky.

"Oh my god, check out her outfit," I said, pointing to the photo. Mariella wore the dorkiest Christmas dress ever. It looked like one of those things a girl would wear at age six—really velvety, with a garish lace bow around the neck and prim lace trim around the sleeves. She carried a ridiculous tiny heart-shaped, lace-trimmed purse.

"We could use this as blackmail," I said, laughing, and that was when I saw another familiar face.

"Look who it is!" I said, pointing.

Emily squinted. In the background of the photo was a scowling man in a V-neck sweater, holding a plate full of cheese and crackers. He wore glasses and had an elaborate mustache.

"Is that . . . the Kaputsa's guy?" Emily said uncertainly.

"Doesn't it look like him?" I said. "I mean, he doesn't have his stupid apron on, but come on! It's definitely him!"

"I wonder if he lives in the building or what," Emily murmured. "Probably needs to be close to Kaputsa's, to be near his precious cheese."

"I've seen him around the neighborhood," I said, narrowing my eyes at the photo.

"I should go soon," Emily said suddenly looking at her watch. "If I get home too late, my mom will kill me. She'll worry that I got trampled by a horse at camp."

"Yeah," I said, "I should probably go too." But I doubted anyone was wondering where *I* was.

Emily heaved herself up. "I have no idea how I'm going to eat dinner," she said, smiling. "Will you invite me back? This place is so cool."

"Of course!" I said.

"And this view is amazing," she went on. "You can see the tops of buildings and stuff! The apartment building across from us has a roof garden up there! I never knew that!" She went over to the CD player to turn it off and gazed dreamily out the window.

"Yeah," I said, putting our cake plates and forks into the sink. Then I remembered that Mipsy was still on the phone with Mrs. W. I picked up the phone. The cat had, as usual, wandered away. But Mrs. W was still talking. I'd left her alone for more than an hour!

"Mrs. W?" I interrupted. "I have to go now. So I'm going to have to hang up."

"Oh, all right," Mrs. W said. "Well, good night, then! And good night, Mipsy!"

Back in the living room, Emily was still looking out the window. "There's something really strange going on across the street," she said.

"On the roof deck?" I said.

"No . . ." She paused. "I don't know. It's . . . on a lower floor. But maybe we shouldn't look. I don't know if it's right to look into other people's windows."

"Okay, now I'm *really* curious," I said.

Emily moved out of the way. "It's in that window, there." She pointed.

I looked out and saw a clearly lit window in the high-rise building across Seventy-second Street. Two people, a man and a woman, stood in front of the window in their kitchen. There were pots and pans hanging on the wall, and a bunch of glasses on the counter. The couple looked pretty young. The woman's hair was in a ponytail, and she wore a sleeveless T-shirt. The guy had glasses, wasn't wearing a shirt, and had a skinny chest. They were screaming at each other. It was easy to tell because the woman's mouth would get very large and the man kept balling his hands into fists.

"Intense," I said.

"I can't believe we can see them so well," Emily said. "I've always heard stories about living in New York City apartments and spying on your neighbors . . . but my apartment faces the park. . . ."

"Mine too," I said.

We continued to watch the couple, even though we felt sort of weird about it. Suddenly, the girl reached down and picked something up. She threw it at the guy. He stepped back, but whatever it was smashed against his face. He took his glasses off and wiped it away.

"What did she throw at him?" I asked.

"It looked like a pie or something," Emily whispered.

"I feel like we shouldn't be doing this," I said. But I couldn't stop watching.

Now the man picked up something in both of his hands and threw it at the woman. It was gooey in the same way. She pulled some of the chunks of the broken pie off her face and whipped it back at him. We could clearly see that he had pie—or whatever it was—pasted in his hair.

Emily scratched her head. "This might be against the law."

"I don't know," I said. I looked across at the line of windows next to the fighting couple's. Many were dark, but it was easy to see right into the windows that were lit. I saw shadowy outlines of other people moving around. I saw one guy sitting on the couch, watching TV, a girl sitting on her bed, putting lotion on her legs, and another person dressed up in a wig and a clown nose, looking at himself in the mirror.

"But it's fun. Like reality TV," Emily said, noticing the other windows too.

"A little *too* real," I said.

Emily moved away from the window. "God, I wish we could come up here during the day tomorrow."

"If only we could ditch camp," I said wistfully.

I thought about it for a minute. I *didn't* want to go back to camp.

"Maybe we *could* sneak out of camp," I said slowly, sitting on a tall-backed living room chair.

"Do you think so?" Emily said.

"There might be a way," I explained. "What if I gave the bus driver a note saying that I was visiting a museum with my mother? He's always trying to be my friend. And Rainbow would definitely approve of that. And since my mother's been leaving for work before the bus comes, I could sneak back into the building without getting caught. Montego would cover for me."

"It's pretty risky," Emily said.

"Yeah, but we have to try," I said. "I don't think I can face camp again."

"But what about me?" Emily said. "What's my excuse?"

"Well . . ." I thought for a minute. "Are there any, um, horse-type events that you could say you're going to?"

"I don't know," Emily said. "I guess I could always say that relatives are in town and want to go to the Museum of Natural History."

"This is great," I said. "We'll both make our excuses, sneak back in, and spend the whole day here!"

Emily was deep in thought. Then she smiled. "What the heck? I can't go back to that horrible camp. Let's ditch!"

"Awesome," I said, feeling a dangerous tingle of nerves run through me as I locked Mrs. W's door.

egg
sammy

Montego
...used to play
the tuba

The next morning, things went according to plan. My mother rushed off to work early because she had to interview someone for a story. I was stuck having breakfast with Mariella, who looked like Minnie Mouse in this ugly, badly fitting red and white polka-dotted top. But she *thought* she looked like a supermodel. I wondered why she was so dressed up. Maybe she was going back to Switzerland!

Mariella chewed slowly on a piece of toast. "You're acting weird this morning," she said, narrowing her eyes.

"I am not," I said. I was trying my hardest to act normal, even though I was nervous about ditching camp.

"Well, you seem like you're up to something," Mariella said.

I just snorted. "Maybe *you're* up to something," I said. "Why are you still here, anyway?" Usually Mariella left for her camp earlier than I did.

"No camp today," she said.

"Why not?" I said.

She glared at me. "None of your business!" She stared at her watch. "But I *am* late for an appointment."

Hmm, was she ditching too? Appointment? I wanted to ask more but was interrupted by her cell phone. Besides, it was time to sneak down to wait for the camp bus a few minutes early so that I could talk to Montego.

He was in the booth as usual. "So listen," I said. "I'm not going to camp today."

"Oh yeah?" He raised an eyebrow and grinned devilishly.

"So . . . can you cover for me? I'll totally owe you," I said.

"You could start paying me back now," Montego said, handing me a five-dollar bill. "How about snagging me an egg-and-cheese sandwich from the deli?"

"You got it," I said, racing down the street.

I got back a few minutes later and handed him the foil-wrapped sandwich. He unwrapped it and took a giant bite. "Mmm," he said. "Thanks. I was starving. So why are you ditching camp?"

He held the sandwich out to offer me a bite, but I shook my head. I was too nervous to eat. "I really need a day off," I explained. "But my mom will kill me if she catches me ditching."

"I won't say a word," Montego said, nearly finished with his sandwich. "When I was your age, my parents made me go to band camp. I had to march around all summer, lugging this stupid tuba, which weighed about a million pounds."

"That sounds awful," I said.

"It was. At first, I thought it was going to be the worst summer ever," he said. "But I actually ended up having a lot of fun that summer, when I *wasn't* at camp."

"Camp is definitely *no fun*," I said. I was glad to have Montego as a friend.

When the camp bus rolled up, I had my forged excuse ready. Fred swung the door open. I climbed up the first step and held out the note. "My mom and I are going to the museums today," I explained.

"You *are*?" I heard a familiar adult voice. *Rainbow* was on the bus! She was sitting in the front seat, next to a six-year-old, holding a Charlie Brown lunch box in her tie-dyed lap. I froze.

"Y-yeah . . . ," I stammered, trying to maintain my composure. "We're, um, going to see some art."

"Fantastic!" Rainbow said. "Which museum?"

"Um . . ." I quickly racked my brain. What were the museums in New York City? I couldn't remember any. "The . . . ," I started groping.

"The Met?" Rainbow coaxed. "The Museum of Natural History?"

"Yes!" I said. "Yes, we're going to both! One today, one tomorrow!" Might as well get myself two camp-free days out of this.

"How exciting! Are you going to look at the Egyptian mummies at the Met?"

"Of course," I said.

"And the undersea exhibit at the natural history museum? Or maybe the woolly mammoth?"

"Uh . . . yeah," I said. "All of it." I felt dizzy. I wasn't a very experienced liar. It always made me nervous to make stuff up. Plus, Rainbow was staring at me so intently.

"Wonderful!" Rainbow said. "Why don't you do some sketches of all those things? You can show it to us in the peace circle!"

"I guess . . . ," I said slowly. Great. What had I gotten myself into? Now I had homework! For camp!

But at least I was free. I stepped off the bus and watched it pull away. The six-year-olds gazed longingly out the window. The thugs in the back punched one another to the beat of Jay-Z.

Emily was waiting for me at Mrs. W's front door. "So I didn't even need an excuse!" she said excitedly. "One of the campers got lice, and she spread it to another kid, and they were afraid of it spreading further, so they gave us the day off!"

"Lice, ew," I said, automatically scratching my head.

"I don't have it," Emily explained. "My mom found out

last night, and she got me checked this morning, before she went to work."

"Good," I said. "I guess I heard something about that from Mariella." I was quiet for a minute. Hopefully Mariella wouldn't be floating around the apartment building today. We'd have to be careful.

"At least you're off the hook," I continued. "*I* have homework!" I told Emily what had happened with Rainbow on the bus.

She paused for a moment. "Well, we *could* sneak out today. It's easy to get to the Met from here—we'll just take the bus!"

"Okay," I said grumpily. That stupid Rainbow. But still, it was better than sitting in the peace circle!

"First let's watch people," Emily said.

"Absolutely," I answered. I unlocked Mrs. W's door. We rooted around in Mrs. W's drawers for a while and found two pairs of binoculars. We dragged our chairs over to the window and looked down onto Seventy-second Street.

"That's the bus I usually take to camp," Emily said, pointing down at a large city bus waiting for the light to change. "But not today!"

I felt a little twinge of worry, thinking of my camp bus rolling up Broadway without me. Sure, I'd gotten off the hook, but what if Rainbow decided to call our house to check up on whether I'd gone to the museums or not? Or what if she ran into my mother on the street? I bit my fingernails a little and thought about the possibility of a babysitter—or worse, Mariella as my babysitter. She'd probably make me iron her bras and pop her pimples or something. Ugh. Maybe ditching camp was a mistake.

Shoving that out of my mind, I turned my attention to the windows across the street. Most of the rooms were dark, and the ones that weren't didn't show anything too interesting. There was a guy who looked to be typing away at a computer, and a woman sitting in an overstuffed armchair watching TV. Emily and I shifted in our seats.

But then I caught sight of two people in clear view, hugging and kissing. They looked young, like teenagers, maybe. I zoomed in for a better view.

"Hey, get a load of the slobber-pusses over there," I said, nudging Emily.

The boy was kind of dorky looking, with baggy jeans, spiky hair, pimples, and a chain wallet loop hanging from his back pocket. He wrapped his arms awkwardly around a skinny girl with long poufy blond hair. It looked like they were kissing in the *kitchen*—there was the stove and the refrigerator! Then the boy turned. Ew. With the binoculars, I could see his tongue. And I could get a better look at the girl. Blond hair, sharp cheekbones, a red and white polka-dotted frilly shirt . . .

I stopped.

"That's Mariella!"

"Noooo!" Emily squealed. "Are you sure?"

"Definitely," I said. "She was wearing that stupid shirt this morning!"

"I know that kid," Emily said, adjusting her binoculars for a closer look. "That's Jason Anderson. He goes to my school. He's lived across the street forever. God, he's such a dork! He's really into Dungeons & Dragons. And when *Lord of the Rings* came out, he went down to the Ziegfeld Theatre dressed like a hobbit! With furry feet and everything!"

"I can't believe *that's* the guy she's been talking about!" I said.

"I know!" Emily said.

Then Emily giggled. "And she doesn't really know how to kiss, does she?"

"She's trying to be all dramatic," I said. Mariella was moving her head around, probably trying to look like someone she'd seen in a movie. I wondered if Michael knew she was across the street, kissing pimply hobbits with chain wallets.

"Jason looks bored!" Emily hooted, pointing. "Wow. This is the first time I've ever seen Jason look cooler than someone."

Now I had two pieces of evidence that I could use to blackmail Mariella—that awful picture of her in that frilly velvet dress from the holiday party, and a view of her sucking face with a boy. Trouble was, I wasn't supposed to be seeing this right now. I was supposed to be at camp. And as for the picture, I probably wasn't supposed to be snooping around in Mrs. W's drawers.

Suddenly, the kissing ended. Mariella and the dorky boy stood apart awkwardly, not sure what to do with their hands. I could see their lips moving and was dying to know what they were saying to each other.

"Mariella looks kind of mad," Emily said.

"He probably told her she's a bad kisser," I said.

Emily laughed.

Mariella looked *really* angry. She turned on her heel and stomped out of the room. The boy followed her, his shoulders hunched.

"Aww, end of show," Emily said.

"Too bad," I said.

I shifted my binoculars over to the next window. There was a guy in his underwear, holding an electric guitar, jumping on his bed!

I thrust my binoculars away. "Gross!" I said.

"The underwear guy?" Emily said. Her binoculars were on her lap. She made a disgusted face and widened her eyes. "Yeah. I just saw that too. I bet he's practicing for when he's going to be onstage with his band at Madison Square Garden. Although it'll never happen. But at least he's not naked."

"Gross!" I said.

"Could you *imagine*?" Emily said. She squinted. "He kind of looks like Montego the doorman, doesn't he?"

"*Noooo*," I said. I looked closer. It wasn't Montego—and after all, he was downstairs.

"Actually," I said, "his face sorta looks like my dad's does in old pictures."

"Really?" Emily said. "So your parents are divorced?"

"No," I said. "My dad, um . . . died. A couple of years ago."

"Oh," Emily said. "I'm really sorry." She was quiet for a minute. "You know, Mariella's mom died too. Her name was Michelle."

"Was she nice?"

Emily paused again. "Yeah, she was. She was very friendly."

The phone rang. Both of us jumped and looked at each other. Mrs. W knew I was at camp during the day, so she probably wouldn't be calling.

"Should we answer?" I whispered. I felt kind of nervous.

"I don't think so," Emily said.

I walked over to the phone. The number came up unlisted. I began to feel prickly. My mother knew I was watching Mrs. W's cat, and maybe she had a sixth sense about me today. I chewed on my pinkie nail.

"Let's see if they leave a message," I murmured. Mrs. W's answering machine clicked on. There was breathing for a moment. But then the caller hung up.

"That was strange," Emily said.

We returned to the windows and I used my binoculars to scan the building across the street. Suddenly, I noticed a window I hadn't seen before.

Through our window, I could see a boy sitting on a stark, plain bed, staring straight at the wall. He looked maybe two or three years older than I was. And his profile was, well, really cute. He looked a little like Justin Timberlake.

Well, no. He had longer hair than Justin Timberlake. But it was wavy and blond. He also reminded me a little of the boy I had a crush on back in Pennsylvania, Dan Connelly. Dan was older and had a tricked-out mountain bike. His father was a painter, so they had huge colorful paintings all over their house. Dan was into silk-screening and print-making, and he always made himself and his friends the coolest T-shirts. Right before I left, he'd made me one with this really neat-looking bee on the front. I felt a little flutter of sadness. I didn't even have his e-mail address.

I adjusted the lenses on the binoculars to zoom in on the boy. There wasn't anything on his walls, and I didn't see a TV. I wondered what he was looking at, and why we hadn't noticed him earlier.

"Come here and look at this guy," I said to Emily.

She walked over to my window. "There," I directed.

"He's cute," Emily said. "I've never noticed that window before."

"He looks really bored," I said.

"Yeah," Emily said. "Wonder what he's doing."

We watched in silence for a few minutes. The guy wasn't moving at all. He wasn't even blinking. I wanted him to turn and face us so we could see him from the front. Maybe he was one of those people who were only cute from the side. He had on Converse All-Star sneakers and wore a bracelet made out of white string on his wrist. His bed looked like a bed in a hospital. White sheets, white pillows.

Emily finally spoke. "You know, I pretty much know all the kids in this neighborhood, but I don't recognize him at all."

"Do you think maybe he's visiting his grandmother or something?" I asked. "Because *that* can't be his bedroom. There's nothing in it! He'd have something cool on the walls, I bet."

Emily turned back to the boy in the window. "I bet he

has a really cool name," she said. "Orlando. Like Bloom. Or Josh. Like Hartnett."

"Or Dan," I said.

"Dan?" she asked. "Who's named Dan?"

I shrugged. "A boy I liked back home." I remembered that right in the middle of Dan's room, he had a big easel, and there was always a new painting on it. I hoped that this guy, whatever his name was, liked art too. Maybe we could draw pictures together. I wondered how I could meet him.

"What do you think he's doing?" I finally said. "Why's he just sitting there?"

"I don't know," Emily said. "Maybe he talked back to his grandmother. Maybe he ate all her prunes and she got mad."

"Maybe he interrupted her while she was watching the Home Shopping Network, and she wasn't able to place her order in time."

We giggled, thinking of various scenarios explaining why Orlando-Josh-Dan was stuck in his room. All of a sudden, he flopped down onto his back and stared up at the ceiling.

"He's really, really cute," Emily said. "But he looks so miserable! I wish we could get his attention."

"It's probably too far away for him to see if we held up a sign," I mused aloud. "He would need binoculars, and I bet Grandma wouldn't get them for him."

"That mean old grannie," Emily giggled. "You know what? I bet she's this mean blue-haired old lady named Bertha McCullers who lives in the neighborhood!"

"Bertha McCullers!" I said. "Even the *name* sounds mean!"

"She pushes people out of line at Kaputsa's and trips little kids with her long cane," Emily explained. "Oh no, Jillian, I *know* it's her! And she's imprisoning our poor Orlando!"

"Dan," I said quietly.

The phone rang again. We looked at each other and then rushed over to the caller ID box. Unlisted. Mrs. W's machine picked up, but this time the caller hung up right away.

Egyptian cat at the Met

The phone stayed quiet for a while. We ate lunch, which consisted of big slices of coconut cake, and then we went downstairs to catch the bus across the park to the Met. That way I could complete my assignment and keep Rainbow happy. Not that I didn't want to go to the Met—I was really excited. I couldn't wait to see all the famous paintings. I just didn't want to be caught—by, say, my mom.

But I felt better when Montego gave us a little nod and a wink as we left.

I'd never been on a New York City bus before. I couldn't believe that Emily was allowed to ride on something so big and scary all by herself. "I've done it for years. It's a piece of cake," she said. But I had more important things to worry about—that phone call. Maybe Rainbow had somehow gotten Mrs. W's number and was on to me? Or worse—my mother was calling. Next stop, Babysitterville.

The huge blue and white bus wheezed up to the stop right across the street from our building, and the doors sighed open. Emily, the veteran, boarded first, swiped her MetroCard, and then swiped it through for me. "Come on," she said, and led me to seats in the middle of the bus.

And whoosh, we were off. I was just about to tell Emily that I hadn't known there was a road in the middle of Central Park when some woman at the back started yelling something at the bus driver. "Turn the air-conditioning off! I'm freezing!" she shouted in a piercingly loud voice.

We turned and saw an old woman with bluish hair that went in a million different directions, a giant quilted bag, and a horrible scowl. She clutched a metal walker as if one of us was going to steal it.

Emily grabbed my hand. "That's Bertha McCullers! The mean old lady I was telling you about!"

"She's definitely mean enough to be the grandma," I whispered.

"Turn the air down!" the woman continued to scream. The bus driver ignored her.

Emily nodded.

"Maybe we could steal her keys or something!" I said. "And break in and free the boy!"

The old woman hissed at us.

"Guh," Emily said. "I'm too afraid of her to steal her keys. I think she's too mean even to be anyone's grandmother."

"Turn the air down!" the woman bellowed again.

Luckily, it was time to get off the bus. To get to the Met, we had to walk about eight blocks uptown on Fifth Avenue. The buildings on this side of the park seemed grander and more private. Sure, the Dakota was grand, but in a dark, Dracula's castle sort of way. I peered into the windows here and saw enormous dining rooms with big sparkly chandeliers and artwork on huge canvases. "Wow," I said, stopping in front of one building, craning my neck to see into the window. On the wall was a painting that looked like a famous one I'd seen once of ballerinas stretching before practice. I had a print of it in one of my art books at home.

I flipped open my sketchbook and pulled out my pen. Quickly, I sketched the ballerinas in the picture. I copied the artwork realistically, as best as I could. I noticed Emily watching me and quickly covered up the drawing.

"It's bad," I said.

"No, it's not!" Emily said. "Come on, let me see."

I raised my hand to show her.

Emily studied it for a moment. I felt nervous; I usually didn't show my stuff to anybody, except for my mom.

"This is great!" Emily finally said. "You have so much talent!"

"Not really," I said modestly.

"No, you do. I can't believe your mom was making you go to that fake camp Pow-Wow art camp. You should be going to a real art place for real artists!"

I finished my sketch and flipped the page. Emily asked to see some of the other drawings, and I reluctantly showed her. Even the ones of Michael and my dad.

"This really looks like Michael," she said. "You're really good!"

Finally, I could see the Met. As we approached it, I broke into a giant smile. Here it was, finally! And it was so beautiful! It was made out of white marble and looked like a giant layer cake, with majestic columns that stretched into the sky.

"Wow," I said.

Inside, the air was cool and refreshing. Emily had her family's membership card, and a minute later we were in the marble hallway. Various rooms opened on all sides. A staircase rose above us.

"What do you need to draw?" Emily whispered.

"I told Rebecca I'd draw the Egyptians," I said.

"Oh, right!" Emily said. "I know where those are. There's a temple and all kinds of crazy tombs and stuff!"

I followed Emily as we passed rooms with old Egyptian art plastered all over the walls. Finally, she pulled me through a long corridor that opened into a gigantic room. On one side were windows that faced a lush garden and behind that, Central Park. At the front of the room was a line of tall stone sculptures—almost like soldiers. Running around the edge of the room was a shallow pond. A lot of people had thrown in pennies and quarters, to make a wish. I dug through my pockets to find some change, but I didn't have any.

It was incredibly quiet in the room, as if the water was absorbing all the noise. People walked in and around the stone hut at the back. And the soldier statues—I realized they were cats—seemed to stare at us.

"Whoa," I said.

"Cool, huh?" Emily said, and pointed to the stone building at the back of the room. "That structure has all these old Egyptian hieroglyphics carved into the walls. It's a temple."

"Wow" was all I could say.

I sat down on a stone seat and began to quickly draw one of the soldier cats. I was glad it wasn't a dog. Emily wandered around. She said she'd been to this museum thousands of times.

But after a few minutes she came running toward me at full speed. "Emergency! Code Red! We gotta get out of here!"

"What?" I said, flipping my sketchbook shut. My heart began to race. "Why?"

"Because!" Emily was out of breath. Her straight brown hair was mussed and her face was flushed. "Because you'll never believe this, but I just saw *Mariella*! In the *hall-way*!" She jutted a thumb to the left.

"*What?*" I asked quietly.

"I swear! With a bunch of kids!"

"Oh no," I said. "If she sees me, she'll totally tell my mom."

"She even has that dog of hers!" Emily said. "She's carrying it in her bag! I can't believe they let her in the museum with him!"

I stood up and looked around quickly. There was nowhere to hide. "Where can we go?" I said. "Is there a back way out?"

"We can cut around this way," Emily said, taking my hand.

Finally, after a lot of running, we were back in the main hall. Mariella was nowhere to be seen.

"Looks like we avoided her," Emily whispered.

"Yeah," I said, unsure. I listened for telltale signs of Ramsay's barks. But nothing. Only the echoes of soft voices and footsteps. I shoved my sketchbook into my bag.

"We'd better get out of here," I said. "I don't want to take any chances."

We burst out into the sweltering heat, onto the Met's wide stone steps. Emily threw her arm against me.

"Don't look to your left," she said very quietly, out of the corner of her mouth.

I snuck a look anyway. There was Mariella, holding Ramsay in her arms, sitting with a bunch of other kids on the steps. Including—I was sure of it—that hobbit dork that she'd been making out with earlier.

"I bet they kicked her out 'cause of that dog," Emily whispered.

"She doesn't go anywhere without him," I whispered back.

"Let's sneak down this way," Emily said.

"Hey!" a voice called.

It sounded like Mariella. A streak of fear ran through me.

Then Ramsay started yipping. "Hey!" the voice cried again. "Come back!"

"Run!" Emily shouted.

And we did.

Orlando
(...through binoculars)

"There's no way she could've seen us," Emily said as we stopped to rest on a bench in the park. I looked around frantically to make sure that Mariella hadn't followed us. But I wasn't too worried about *that*; Mariella certainly wasn't the type who would break into a gallop after me. Especially if she was wearing her red pointy-toed shoes and carrying Ramsay. There was a big reservoir right in front of us. Even though it was a hundred billion degrees outside, people were jogging around the reservoir on a gravel track.

"But she was yelling at us!" I said.

"We don't even know if that was her voice for sure," Emily said. "Let's just get back into the building before she does. It'll be fine."

We made it across the park quickly and were back in Mrs. W's apartment in a few minutes.

"You'll never believe this," Emily said, standing at the window. "Orlando is *still* sitting on the bed!"

"No!" I said, and bolted over next to her. There was the cute boy, sitting on the bed.

"That's so sad," Emily said. "I wonder if he's in trouble or something. I wonder if he needs to be rescued."

"I think we have a phone call situation, too," I said, heading over to the answering machine. The light was blinking furiously, and the machine said that Mrs. W had twelve messages. I pressed the Playback button—Mrs. W. had asked me to check her messages for her while she was away.

Twelve silences, twelve hang-ups. And on the caller ID, the same unlisted phone number. In the background of one of the messages, I heard a *tweedly-tweedly-tweedle* cell phone ring. . . .

Either Mrs. W got a lot of phone calls from telemarketers, or somebody was on to us.

o o o

Luckily, Mariella had plans with her friends for dinner. When she got home, I pretended to be asleep.

But I wasn't so lucky the next morning at breakfast. Mariella sat opposite me, wearing a teeny denim skirt and a bright red tank top, chewing loudly on a withered piece of toast with just the tiniest bit of butter on it. I nearly covered my ears.

At one point, she looked up and glared at me. "Enjoying camp?" she asked smirking.

"Um, yeah," I said.

"You think you're so smart," she whispered.

My heart froze. "What are you talking about?" I said, as nonchalantly as possible.

"You can't fool me." She put down her slice of toast and started admiring her fingernails. "Come here, Ramsay!" Her little dog clicked over to her feet and, in one smelly leap, jumped onto her lap.

"I don't know what I can't *fool* you about," I said. "And get that disgusting dog away from me." I avoided her gaze. If Mariella thought I'd been ditching, she couldn't prove anything. She'd been way over on the other side of the stairs at the Met. Even if she'd had superhero vision, she wouldn't have been able to tell for sure that it was Emily and me. Besides, it might not have been her voice the day before at all, but someone else's . . . she was probably too caught up in that stupid boy . . .

I snorted, thinking about Mariella's lousy kissing.

"What's so funny?" she said, her eyes widening. Ramsay scowled.

"Oh, nothing," I said in a singsongy voice.

"I'm late for my tae kwon do lesson," she said haughtily.

"Tae kwon do?" I mumbled.

"Yes," my mother said, waltzing into the room, scaring

me half to death. "Mariella takes tae kwon do with a famous sensei, isn't that right? At the sports club on Sixty-seventh?"

Mariella shrugged. "My father says I should take martial arts so I can defend myself on the subway and stuff. *And* he'll buy me more treatments at the Reebok spa."

"Don't *you* have camp?" I said. Maybe Mariella was ditching too.

"There was a lice outbreak, so no camp," Mariella said.

Duh. Emily and Mariella went to the same camp. I'd forgotten. I stuck my tongue out at her.

"I hear you're really good at tae kwon do! Like a black belt!" my mother continued, not noticing my look. Gag. She was totally *drooling* over stupid Mariella.

Michael breezed into the room, carrying his briefcase and a mug of coffee. "She's been taking it for five years, so she's *past* a black belt by now," he said.

"Yeah, I'm good," Mariella said obnoxiously. She scooped Ramsay up off her lap and set him back down on the floor. "I'm probably the best in the class." She gave me a dangerous look, as if to say, *You'd better watch out because I'll hurt you.*

"Jillian, would you like to take tae kwon do too?" my mother asked.

"You girls could go together!" Michael added.

"Uh, no," I said. Tae kwon do sounded nearly as bad as camp. Besides, the only person I needed to defend myself against was Mariella.

My mother rushed out of the apartment with Michael. "I'm late," she said. "Have fun at camp!"

"I will!" I called. Mariella was standing around in the hall. Was she waiting for me? As slowly as I could, I gathered up my backpack and sketchbook. I bent over and tied my shoes. *Leave!* I screamed inwardly. But Mariella just stood there, seemingly waiting for me. I pretended the bow on my shoe was really hard to tie.

"Aren't you going to miss your bus?" Mariella said.

"No," I said. "It waits for me if I'm late."

Mariella snorted.

After tying and retying my shoe about six times, I stood up. Mariella smirked. "Ready?" she asked.

"Okay," I said. "Er, no! I have to go to the bathroom."

"No! You can't, you'll be late to camp!" Mariella said sweetly. "Why don't you just hold it?" As if she actually cared! I gritted my teeth and walked through the door.

"But Mariella," I said, in an equally fake sweet voice. "I thought you said *you* were late."

"I *am*," she said, pushing the elevator's Down button. "But I didn't want to leave you alone in the house! You're too young, after all!"

"I am not!" I screeched. "How old do you think I am? I've stayed alone in the house before."

"Your mother told me to keep an eye on you," she said primly. "Since I *am* the older one."

"You don't *act* older!" I yelled.

The elevator dinged and the doors slid open. I stamped inside. But Mariella paused. A scowl settled over her face.

"I left my workout clothes in my room," she said. "Will you hold the elevator? I'll just run back in."

I smiled and quickly pushed the Door Close button.

"Hey!" I heard her call as the doors closed. Whew! A lucky break! I got down to the courtyard, where I had to change elevators to get to Mrs. W's. I felt my stomach turn and I shivered. Mariella was on to me, for sure. I wondered if *she* was calling Mrs. W's house and hanging up. If I'd had her cell phone, I could have proved it. But there was no way I'd be able to wrench her phone out of her hands for even a second.

I'd narrowly escaped this time. Emily and I had to watch our backs.

o   o   o

"I'm glad you're here," Emily said when I got to Mrs. W's front door. "When you were late, I thought you might've gotten roped into going to camp!"

"Almost," I said, and explained what had happened with Mariella. "And I think she might be the one calling and hanging up."

"Are you sure?" Emily said. "Maybe it's just some friend of Mrs. W's. There's no way Mariella saw us yesterday."

"That's fine, but we should be careful today," I said. "I think I told Rainbow I'd do something about a woolly mammoth. Is there some kind of woolly mammoth exhibit at the natural history museum?"

"Oh yeah! The woolly mammoth!" Emily was practically jumping up and down. "He's so cool. He has giant bones!"

"I made a face. "How am I going to draw that?" Drawing bones sounded hard.

She thought for a minute. "Maybe you could take

pictures instead, like a photography project. Mrs. W has a Polaroid camera in the kitchen."

"Maybe," I said, finally getting the door unlocked.

We burst into the apartment and headed straight to the window. Emily saw him first. "No way," she said. "Look!"

She pointed. The cute boy was still sitting on the bed, staring at the wall. His hair was messier, and he was wearing the same T-shirt.

"Do you think maybe there's something *wrong* with this kid?" I slowly asked Emily as we watched. "What kind of boy stays in his room all the time, staring at the wall?"

"I don't know," Emily answered. "It doesn't *seem* like there's anything wrong with him. It just seems like he . . . I don't know . . . like he's being punished for something."

"Maybe," I said. I thought for a minute. "Do you think . . . do you think there's a possibility that he was *kidnapped*?"

"Kidnapped!" Emily's eyes widened.

Being kidnapped was a million times more exciting than being punished. We started to concoct a story of what had happened. "He was living downtown, in the West Village," Emily began in a very stage-polished voice.

"Where's that?" I said.

"It's this cool little neighborhood downtown," she explained. "Lots of winding, twisty streets, little cafés and shops, and lots of cute dogs."

"Oh," I said, and tried to smile.

"So anyway," Emily went on. "He was hanging out in Washington Square Park one day, acting totally cute, maybe auditioning for a movie role. Or maybe he was riding his bike around the park, doing tricks on the ramps."

"Or maybe he was sitting on the grass, making silk screens," I said, thinking again about Dan, my old crush from home.

"Yeah, something like that," Emily said. "So . . ."

"Hold that thought," I said, peering at the boy with my binoculars. "I think I want to sketch him." I ran to get my sketchbook and pencil and opened the book to a clean page. I made swift lines for his jaw and forehead. Then his nose, then the indentation of his eyes. "Go on," I said.

"So, he's minding his own business, about to become the next big movie star, and . . . all of a sudden . . . one of the snake handlers comes up and snatches him away!"

"Snake handlers?" I said, stopping my sketching to look up at her.

"Yeah, they're these guys in the park who walk around with these big nine-foot-long boa constrictors around their necks. They're *crazy*. I bet they kidnap tons of kids— and feed them to the snakes!"

"Oh no!" I said. "And I bet Orlando"—I gestured toward him—"tastes *extra good* to a snake because he's so cute!"

"Absolutely," Emily said. "So the snake handler threw him into a yellow cab and then got in himself—snake and all— and they came all the way up here, to the Upper West Side!"

I loved the dramatic way Emily told the story. "I bet the snake handler's really ugly," I said.

"Yeah, he has a spike through his nose," Emily said. "Sometimes it stabs him when he sneezes!"

We burst into laughter. I looked down and filled in the shadows of the boy's cheeks and eyes. "And I bet he was once the prince of a country," I said, "but then . . . but then something happened to the country!"

"It sank into the ocean," Emily said knowingly. "But you know what? His only loyal subjects in the country were snakes!"

I snorted with laughter. "So . . . ," I giggled, trying to get my thought out, " . . . so that's why he came to New York, to hang out in the park!"

Even though the story was completely silly, it threw us into hysterics. Emily looked at my drawing of Orlando. "I can't believe you can draw like that," she said. "I'm so impressed. It looks just like him."

"Nahh," I said. "It doesn't really at all. I messed up his eyes."

"No way, Jillian, this is wonderful." She looked at me and smiled. "Can I have it?"

"Sure," I said, shrugging. I ripped the drawing of the boy out of my sketchbook and gave it to her.

"You've got to sign it!" Emily said. So I signed my name messily at the bottom. I'd only seen artists sign their paintings with a weird scribble, so I was working to perfect an artist's signature of my own.

As soon as I'd added a squiggly flourish at the bottom of my name, the doorbell rang. Or at least I *thought* it was the doorbell. It was a loud noise that sounded like it had come from one of those gongs you sometimes see at Chinese restaurants.

Emily and I froze and looked nervously at each other.

The gong sounded again.

"Should we answer it?" I whispered, putting down my sketchbook.

"I don't know," Emily whispered back.

"Maybe we could see who it is?" I said.

"But what if it's your *mom*?"

I began to bite my fingernails.

"You look," I said to Emily as we slithered ever so quietly up to the door.

"No, you!" she said.

But I shoved Emily up toward the peephole. For a split second, she glanced through it, and then she crouched back down on the floor.

"No one was there!" she whispered.

"Are you sure?" I stood up and looked. But she was right; no one was there.

I slumped back to the floor, my heart racing and my palms sweaty. Even though we hadn't seen anyone, I had a feeling I knew who our visitor was—Mariella.

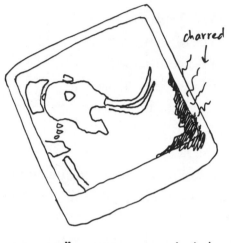

charred

woolly mammoth skeleton

"**H**ow are we going to get out to go to the museum?" I asked, pacing around. "I need something to show Rainbow."

"You think Mariella is still lurking outside the door?" Emily asked.

"I don't know, but I don't want to risk it. Is there another way out?" We were up way too high to go out the window.

"Wait! What about the service elevator?" Emily asked.

"The service elevator," I said slowly. Every apartment

in the building had access to a second elevator that delivery people used. I'd never been inside it, but it was an idea.

"Mariella wouldn't think to look for us there," Emily added.

We called down to Montego to make sure we could use the elevator without getting stuck. "Sure, you can use it," he said. "But what are you girls up to?"

"We're trying to hide from Mariella," I explained. "I think she knows I'm skipping camp!"

"Aha," Montego said. "I saw her not too long ago, coming back from that martial arts class she goes to. She didn't see me watching her, but before she came inside the building, she was standing at the curb, talking on her cell phone, looking real upset!"

Upset? What did Mariella have to be upset about? That boy? "So she's in the building now?" I asked.

"As far as I know," Montego said.

We crept out Mrs. W's back door and into a very narrow hallway. We pushed the Elevator Call button and heard the elevator slowly creaking up. When the door slid open, I was surprised to see how old-fashioned it was. You had to pull open a little door and then slide back a grate just to get inside!

It dropped us off in a discreet hallway next to the Dakota's lobby. "We're making a secret escape!" Emily whooped, scooting out into the street.

We walked quickly up Central Park West. Emily stopped me after a few blocks. "Did you bring money?" she asked. "The museum is six dollars, I think, and I'm not a member."

"No," I said. "And I'd be too nervous to go back inside to get some." Usually I carried around a little bit of money, for an ice cream cone from the truck, or in case Mipsy needed more cat food. But just my luck, I hadn't brought any with me today.

"Maybe we could sneak into the museum!" Emily said.

"Are you serious?" I said uncertainly. After the freaky ding-dong-ditch incident (I just *knew* it was Mariella), I'd had just about enough danger for one day already.

"Sure!" Emily said. "I used to sneak into the museum a lot when I was younger. It's really, really easy. You just slip past the guards when they're not looking!"

"Did you ever get caught?" I said. My bag, which held Mrs. W's Polaroid camera, kept slamming me in the thigh. Emily didn't answer.

We finally got to the museum and went inside. "This way," Emily said quietly, leading me along a wall. Through a large doorway, I could see a fleet of elephants standing on a pedestal in the middle of a large room. For a second, I thought they were real.

Emily's eyes suddenly lit up. "We're in luck!" she said. She pointed to a large cluster of kids by the doors. "A big group! Probably a camp, or a church group or something!"

At the word *camp,* I swung my head around, my heart hammering. But luckily, the group of kids wasn't from Camp Powanasett. Many had green T-shirts with CAMP CHAPPAQUA emblazoned on the back. Most looked as miserable as I had been.

"We can blend in with them!" Emily urged, her eyes wide. She grabbed my hand. "Come on!"

We moved into the center of the clump. No one even noticed us. Then we started moving with the group toward the elephant room. "We're going in!" Emily whispered. She was pretty excited about sneaking in. I, on the other hand, was beyond nervous. What if we got caught and the police hauled us away to jail? We'd have to call our parents to bail us out, and we'd be in huge trouble. At the very least, I'd have to go back to camp, and Rainbow would probably make up a song about me, using her bongo. I swallowed hard.

"Keep up with them!" Emily whispered. "Come on!"

We moved through the lobby and past the guard. I held my breath and ducked my head. We were inside! Emily nudged me. "We're in the clear now! Better get away from this crowd before they wonder who we are," she said.

I nodded doubtfully.

She led me down some corridors, up a flight of stairs, and into another giant room.

In this room were the huge bones of all sorts of extinct, prehistoric things—including the woolly mammoth. "Wow," I whispered, looking at drawings on the wall of the giant beasts. "Look at its tusks."

"Scientists are trying to clone the woolly mammoth and bring him back by the year 2025," Emily said dramatically, reading the plaque next to the exhibit and then looking closely at the mammoth's skeleton. Her eyes widened. "Isn't that *spooky*?"

I was feeling spooked just being in this room. The museum was pretty deserted; that big group of kids had gone in another direction. We were alone with all these bones." It's like he's *looking* at me," I whispered, gesturing to the woolly mammoth skeleton. "Even though he doesn't have eyes!"

"Maybe he's still alive," Emily said in a low, scary voice.

The mammoth loomed over me. Uneasy, I held my camera up to take a picture. I was a little afraid that he was going to knock the camera out of my hands with his big tusk. My hands shook. Be brave, I told myself. Emily was going to think I was a huge wimp if I didn't suck it up and take a picture.

So I pressed the button. *Snap!* "What a flash!" Emily said, covering her eyes. "God, that thing's blinding! And it smells like it's burning!"

"Yeah, and the picture isn't coming out!" I said. I could hear whirring inside the camera, but it sounded like the gears were rusty. "Maybe it's broken or something!"

Then, with a groan, the Polaroid finally decided to spit out the picture, right onto the floor. I screamed and, my sneakers squealing across the marble floor, bolted out of the room.

I didn't stop until I'd passed the elephants again, run to the exit, burst out onto the front steps, and was back on the sidewalk on Central Park West.

Emily followed me a split second later, laughing. "You should've seen your face!" she hooted. "That was awesome!"

"I don't know," I said. "Sneaking in, the woolly mammoth, the smell . . ."

"Well, you forgot this," Emily said, handing me the picture. I looked at it. The woolly mammoth had come out all blurry. My hand must really have been shaking when I took the picture.

I burst out laughing. "This is the worst picture ever!" I said. "I can't show this to Rainbow!"

"Well, I gotta tell you, Jillian," Emily said. "You're a real New Yorker now. You've snuck into your first museum—and survived!"

"Yeah," I said, smiling a little. "I guess I did."

o   o   o

When we got back to the Dakota, Montego flagged us down. "Watch out," he whispered. "Mariella's right over there by the fountain!"

Sure enough, there was Mariella in profile, talking on her cell phone. There was no way past her.

"She's been on the phone down here for about ten minutes now," Montego said.

"She looks pretty upset," Emily murmured.

It was true: Mariella's face was all puffy, and her mouth was turned down. After a few minutes, I realized she was crying.

"You can hide in my booth with me until she's gone," Montego whispered. "Come on, quick."

We all squeezed into Montego's booth, which was kind of ridiculous, because it was only big enough for one really skinny person. I could hardly breathe. I kept poking my head out and watching Mariella on the phone. Who was making her so upset?

Suddenly she let out a wail. "But I miss her! I miss her so much!"

Emily and I looked at each other. *Her?* I'd thought Mariella was bummed out about that stupid guy from across the street. We both shrugged. Montego hadn't heard her; he was busy helping a lady with her fifty shopping bags into the building.

A few minutes later, Mariella got off the phone and wandered, sniffling, onto the street. We ducked down in Montego's booth so she wouldn't see us. A strange feeling washed over me. Who did Mariella miss? What was she talking about? It was pretty sad to see someone cry like that. Even if she *was* your worst enemy.

We rode the service elevator back up. When we got to Mrs. W's, we had just enough time to check on Orlando. Still there, looking more miserable than ever. "I guess Slade the snake handler hasn't fed him again today," Emily said.

But we didn't laugh about it this time. Something seemed wrong. It seemed like the cute boy *was* imprisoned. For real.

Mariella...
is on to me

12

When I unlocked the door of my own apartment, it was dark; it seemed like no one else was home yet. I dropped my sketchbook in my bedroom and wandered uneasily through the kitchen. The cute boy hadn't left the room in the apartment across the street for two days. And he seemed really upset. From Mrs W's window, Emily and I were the only two people who had a direct view into the boy's room.

Had he been kidnapped?

I went into Michael's little office. In it was a Mac with a flat-screen monitor. I hadn't used it yet, but my mom had given me the password in case I ever wanted to log on to the Internet. I thought maybe I could go online to find out whether anyone in the city had been kidnapped recently.

I sat down at the desk, turned on the computer, and stared out the window. The little room faced the Dakota's inner courtyard. I could see right into someone's window across the way. A woman stood at her stove, cooking and talking on the phone. It seemed that in New York, people didn't even notice or care that you could see them.

I logged on to the Internet. But after doing a quick search on Web sites for the big city papers—the *New York Times* and the *Post,* and for NY1, the city's local TV news channel—I came up with nothing.

Frustrated, I checked my e-mail. There was a message from my friend Andie back home, telling me that Dan had asked about me the day before. I smiled but then felt a twinge of sadness. I'd probably never see him again.

Then I noticed an e-mail from an address I didn't recognize: turtledove2111@yahoo.com. I opened it. To my surprise, it was Rainbow. We'd written down our e-mail addresses and phone numbers that first day at camp, but she didn't seem like the computer type.

The e-mail said:

Dear Jillian,
I left a message on your home phone but thought

I'd send you a little note, too. I hope everything went OK at the Met and the Museum of Natural History! I can't wait to see your drawings!!! We have some exciting exercises coming up! Hint: dancing with scarves and handbells!
Peace and love, Rainbow

Scarves and handbells!

Wait a second.

She tried my *home phone*?

I looked at the date and time. She'd written the e-mail that day, about three hours earlier. My heart started to pound. I scraped back my chair and ran to the answering machine, which was in the kitchen. The red light was blinking. Whew. If Rainbow *had* left a message, the light meant no one had listened to it yet. I pressed the Playback button on the machine, and then heard the sound of a key in the lock.

Someone was home! I looked frantically at the answering machine. The machine's voice told me that I had two new messages. I heard the jiggling doorknob—whoever was home was having a hard time getting the door open. The first message was from some friend of Michael's who had a question about finding the best caterer in the neighborhood. I quickly hit a bunch of buttons, and happily the machine called out, "Message skipped."

The stupid machine voice was now saying, "Message two" incredibly slowly. "Hurry *up!*" I said through my teeth. I heard the familiar tap of strappy sandals. *Mariella!*

Message two *was* from Rainbow. "Hi, Jillian!" her voice chirped. I searched for the Delete button, but couldn't find it. I pushed the same buttons as I had before, and nothing happened. This stupid answering machine was a different model than the one I'd had in my old house in Pennsylvania. It looked like something you'd have on a space shuttle, with a bunch of futuristic, unlabeled buttons! Luckily, Mariella must have stopped to look at the mail.

Rainbow continued: "I was just calling to check how the museums were today, and . . ."

There was the Delete button! It was hidden on the side of the machine! I pressed it a million times. Rainbow's voice stopped. The machine said in a bored voice, "Message two has been deleted."

"What's going on?" came an amused voice behind me.

I turned. There was Mariella, holding a shopping bag that said SCOOP.

"Nothing," I said.

"You're home a little bit early, aren't you?"

I checked the clock: it was 6:20. "Nope," I said. "I got off the camp bus about twenty minutes ago."

"You're such a liar," Mariella said. "You're not going to camp, and I know it."

I shivered. "Of course I'm going to camp," I said.

"Oh yeah? Then who was that message from? I bet it was from your counselor or something. Am I right?"

I gritted my teeth. How did she *know*? "It was from my friend from home," I said feebly.

"Whatever," Mariella said. "You know what I think? I think you're hanging out at that crazy lady's penthouse all day. Did the doorbell happen to ring today, perhaps?"

I flinched. It *had* been Mariella at the door! "I don't know what you're talking about," I said. "I was at camp all day today. We had field day in the park, and we played kickball."

"Kickball, my butt," Mariella said, giving me an incredulous look. "I don't believe you for one second."

"Leave me alone!" I cried.

"Girls," my mother said. I jumped. She was holding a big bag of groceries from Kaputsa's. Michael stood beside her. I hadn't heard either of them come in. "What's going on?"

"Oh, nothing, Karen!" Mariella said sweetly. She was *such* a fake. I bared my teeth at her back. My mother raised her eyebrows in warning.

"Jillian was just telling me about camp!" Mariella continued.

"Really?" my mother said. She looked doubtful. "Are you having fun there?" she asked, tilting her head a little. "What do they have you doing?"

"Art stuff," I muttered.

Michael coughed awkwardly. "I ran into Robert today," he said. "And he said he didn't see you in the art class today. Are you on a special project?"

My mouth went dry. Mariella snorted. Okay, think fast, I told myself. I could tell them I was at the Museum of Natural History, but if they wanted to check, they might find out that I'd snuck in. Was there a way of finding that out?

"Well?" my mother prompted, putting the bag down on the kitchen counter.

"I, um, I went to the Whitney," I said, pulling out of the air the name of a museum that I knew absolutely nothing about.

"Really!" Michael said excitedly. He began putting the groceries away. I noticed they'd bought a gigantic wheel of cheese. Blegh. "You're kidding! How sophisticated!"

Mariella screwed up her face and rolled her eyes.

"Yeah," I said. "It's kind of a special project. Because . . . I'm interested in, um, Whitney's art."

I had no idea if Whitney was an artist or who exactly he or she was. I hoped no one would notice.

"So . . . what did you see there?" my mother asked. She pulled out a big loaf of French bread and tore off a hunk.

"I . . . uh . . . some photography," I said.

"How wonderful!" my mother continued, offering Mariella the loaf. Mariella shook her head and stomped out of the room. I was glad to see her go.

"Did you draw anything?" Michael asked. "Robert's told me that when campers go on trips to the museums, they always bring back sketches of what they've seen. I bet you made some great drawings!"

Luckily, my mother offered me the bread next, and I tore off a gigantic piece and shoved it into my mouth. I tore off another piece and rolled it into a ball between my hands, as if it was clay. There. Now my mouth was too full to talk.

But my mother didn't care. "Well, did you do any drawings?"

"I . . . I did," I said. "But, um, they're at camp."

"Will you bring them home tomorrow? I'd love to see them."

"Sure," I mumbled. This would mean I'd have to go to the Whitney, wherever it was. At least it was another excuse for Rainbow.

I stomped back to my room, feeling more and more trapped. The cute boy and I had something in common, I thought angrily.

But my bedroom door was closed. I put my hand on the knob—I didn't care if Mariella was in there or not. My sketchbook was in my bedroom, and I wanted to take it for a ride on the Dakota elevators. But I heard a small voice from inside and stopped.

"I just miss her so much, Aunt Beth . . . ," Mariella was saying in a thick voice. I was pretty sure Aunt Beth was the aunt she had been visiting in Switzerland. "Karen is nice, but she's not like Mom."

I backed away from the door. My mouth dropped open. Her mom? I felt a twinge of pain. Mariella missed her *mom*. Kinda like I missed my dad.

"It's just hard . . . ," Mariella went on. "And that snot-nosed Jillian isn't making it any easier. I just *know* she's ditching camp. Once I find out for sure, I'm going to bust her so bad! Maybe then they'll send her away to boarding school or something and I'll be rid of her."

What? The tiny bit of sympathy I'd just had for Mariella disappeared.

I whirled around and stomped out the door, leaving my sketchbook where it was. "Be home in half an hour for dinner!" my mother called after me. I slammed the door without answering her. I had a feeling I wouldn't be very hungry.

bow tie too small for neck

itching to punch somebody

Bulldog

The next day, I met Emily up at Mrs. W's. And I met her the day after that, too. The more days I spent away from camp, the more I couldn't imagine going back. I kept e-mailing Rainbow and telling her I was visiting different museums, and she believed me. Lying through e-mail was much easier than lying in person. I made sure to check the answering machine during the day from Mrs. W's house just in case Rainbow called, and when she did, I was able to delete her messages.

Emily's camp still had the lice epidemic, so she happily went with me to the museums. We ate more of Mrs. W's cakes and played on the potter's wheel, and I made a really cool pastel drawing of Emily sitting on Mrs. W's window seat. We continued to get hang-up phone calls from Mariella. But mostly, we checked on Orlando. Same bed, same closed door, same everything. I sketched him obsessively: sitting up, profile, front view, lying down.

One day we noticed he was eating something. "It looks like hard-boiled eggs," Emily said.

"No, it looks yuckier than that," I said, watching him wince as he raised the fork to his mouth. "Smushier. Definitely tofu."

"Imagine having to eat tofu for the rest of your life," Emily said sadly.

"Yuck," I said.

"We need to get into the building," I said as I colored in a sketch of Orlando with his chin tipped toward the ceiling. "And then we could go to his apartment and see what's going on!"

"That building's impossible to get into," Emily said.

"Even for a master sneak like you?" I joked. But I wasn't totally kidding.

"No, seriously. I used to have a friend who lived in that building. The doorman *hates* kids. His name's Bulldog. I heard he threw this kid from Seventy-eighth Street out of the building *on his ear.*" Her eyes widened.

"Really?" I said. "Why's he so mean?"

"I don't know," she said. "He's a bigmouth. He tells on

kids in his building all the time. If they're late, if they're hanging around on the street, whatever, he tells the parents. Bulldog knows everyone and everything. I bet he knows Michael. He'd probably call up Michael and say he saw you in the building, and bam! You'd be busted."

"Wow," I said. "Well, maybe we could go on Saturday, when we're not supposed to be at camp."

"Yeah," Emily said. "But it's only Monday. Orlando could be dead by then! And besides, even if Bulldog doesn't tell on us, he still won't let us in the building."

"This is just awful," I said. It was all so complicated and confusing. I sat and thought for a minute. "You know, we really don't *know* what's going on there. I mean, we've never actually *seen* kidnappers in Orlando's room. And sure, he's there all the time that *we're* here. But we're not here all the time. Maybe he just hangs out all day because he doesn't have anything else to do and he leaves after we go to sleep! I mean, we have no idea what goes on when we're not at the window!" I tried to sound optimistic, but it came out sounding squeaky.

Emily looked concerned. "Maybe he leaves at night. Or maybe nighttime is when the kidnappers come and, y'know, torture him."

Emily and I looked at each other. And then we both looked at the floor. We sat there for what seemed like years, not talking. My stomach hurt and I bet hers did too.

"Maybe we could watch from Mrs. W's tonight, just to see?" I ventured. It probably wouldn't be too hard to sneak up to Mrs. W's when everyone was sleeping.

o o o

Getting out of my own apartment was going to be tricky. I lay in bed, facing the wall, waiting out Mariella and her cell phone conversation.

"He and I went to Tasti D-Lite last week, and he said we could go to Barney's this weekend and he'd buy me something!" she gushed.

It sounded like she was back with the hobbit guy. At around twelve-thirty, I heard her even, soft breaths. She'd finally fallen asleep with the cell phone held against her ear. I was very careful not to make a sound as I got out of bed.

I tiptoed down the hall and out the front door. I went down the one elevator and up the other elevator and met Emily at Mrs. W's door. We went inside, but we didn't turn on any lights, in case the kidnapper came into Orlando's room. We didn't want him to see us, across the street, spying on him. We didn't say a word to each other until we were safely inside the apartment, looking out the windows.

"Maybe he's dead," Emily whispered. The binoculars were up to her face and she was looking across Seventy-second Street into Orlando's window. His room was softly lit by a lamp in the corner. Orlando was splayed out on the bed.

"No, I think I just saw him move," I whispered back, looking through my own binoculars.

"I can't see what's going on," Emily said, frustrated. She put down her binoculars and sighed. "Look, we can spend every day and every night watching him through this window, but we're never really going to know what's going on unless we ask him ourselves. I've been thinking about it a lot. We have to get inside that building."

"But what about Bulldog?" I said, gulping.

"Maybe there's another doorman on duty right now," Emily said. "Come on . . . let's at least *try!*"

"All right," I said. I knew Emily was right. What choice did we have?

In the elevator, I sat down on the little plush seat. I was pretty nervous and wanted to change the subject. "Remember when we heard Mariella on the phone in the lobby?"

"Yeah," Emily said.

"Well, I heard her talking about the same thing again later that night. But this time I heard more. And she was . . . she was talking about her mom. And how she was sad and missed her and stuff."

Emily was quiet. "You guys are kinda the same," she said. "Both of you had a parent who died."

"Yeah," I mumbled.

Emily turned toward me. "You know, you never talk about your dad," she said. She tipped her head to the side. "You must miss him a lot."

Truth was, it was sort of hard to talk about my dad to someone who hadn't also lost their mom or dad. I remembered trying to talk about it to my friend Andie when it happened, when I was nine. But she'd just acted confused, like she didn't really understand what *dead* meant, and how important and terrible it was.

Downstairs, Montego was on duty. "What's up?" he asked, grinning, and offering us his bag of potato chips. When he saw our confused looks—we'd seen him that morning, and what, did he *live* at the bottom of the Dakota?—he explained, "I'm working a double shift today because I want to go to the baseball game this weekend."

"Cool," I said, taking a chip. "So we're trying to get into the building across the street," I said.

"Is Bulldog working?" Emily asked. I guessed everyone in the neighborhood knew him by that name.

"I think he is," Montego said.

"Then forget it," I whispered to Emily. "I don't want to get thrown out on my ear!"

"But if you want," Montego said, "I could call him, maybe. And distract him, and you could sneak past? Me and him are friends, sort of."

I looked at Emily. "That might work," I said. I asked Montego, "What would you talk to him about?"

"The Boston Red Sox," Montego said. When we both looked confused, he explained, "Bulldog is a diehard Yankees fan. Whenever someone talks to him about the Boston Red Sox—they are the Yankees' biggest rivals—he goes crazy."

I looked at Emily. "It's true," she said. "The Red Sox and the Yankees fans hate each other. My father is a Sox fan and my mom's a Yankees fan. It can get pretty ugly at our house when the two teams are playing each other."

Montego picked up the phone and dialed. Emily and I scampered out onto the quiet street.

"It's totally different down here at night," I said softly. The city was so loud and busy during the day, but now, I felt like I could whisper and still be heard. It smelled a lot better at night too. With the moon bright in the sky and the streetlights making yellow circles on the sidewalk, it actually looked kind of pretty.

We edged across the street to the building's door, keeping close to the wall. Moving slowly toward the lobby, we peered inside. Emily pulled back quickly.

"That's him!" she whispered. "That's Bulldog!"

I took another look. Bulldog stood just past the door. He was bald and had a gruff look on his face. He wore a small hoop earring in one ear, like a meaner version of Mr. Clean. He stood perfectly still, arms crossed over his chest, protecting the building.

We could hear the phone ringing behind him, but for some reason he was ignoring it.

"Why isn't he answering the phone?" I said.

I looked across the street. Montego still had the phone to his ear. He saw me watching him and shrugged.

"Well, if he won't pick up the phone, there's no way we can sneak past him!" Emily said.

I put my hand over my own ear. "We should go back, then," I said. "This'll never work."

"I guess you're right," Emily said. "We'll have to think of another way."

A newspaper box on the street already had the papers for the next day. The headline read LOCAL BOY KIDNAPPED, RANSOM NOTE FOUND.

I stopped and stared. Oh no. This could not be real. This could *not* be real.

But it was. The picture of the boy on the cover was the spitting image of the boy in the apartment!

"Emily!" I whispered, pulling her over.

"Kidnapped," she mouthed. "That's . . ." She trailed off.

Neither of us had any money, so we couldn't buy a paper. The picture looked like the kind from school. Orlando's hair was combed, his face looked clean, and he had on a shirt and tie. But still, having drawn him so many times, I knew the contours of his face by heart. I had no doubt that it was the same boy. I breathed in and grabbed Emily's arm. She was shaking.

"How is this . . . ," Emily said. "I mean, we were just kidding. I thought . . . I didn't really . . ." Her voice rose to a nervous high pitch.

Emily and I had been *right.*

"What do we do?" she finally said.

"I don't know," I said. But then I heard a familiar voice behind me.

I turned slowly and flinched. There was Mariella, leaning against the very same building in which the kidnappers were holding Orlando. She stared right at us.

With her was that dorky boy we'd seen her kissing almost two weeks before.

Mariella strode toward us before I could run. "What do you think you're doing?" she asked nastily. "I noticed you weren't in bed, so I came down here to find you. Why are you guys reading the paper in the box? Why don't you go up to that freaky woman's apartment and read it there?"

I made a little squeaky noise at the back of my throat. The dorky kid snorted but didn't say anything.

"We don't go there!" Emily said, too quickly.

"Oh yeah, like you're not there during the day?" Mariella said. "The building has video cameras on every floor. They have you on tape, going into Mrs. Whiteflower's apartment *after* you were supposed to be on the camp bus! And I've seen the tape!"

My eyes widened. Was this *true*? "Montego would never . . . ," I said.

"It wasn't Montego, stupid," Mariella said. "He's not the *only* doorman in the building. It was someone else. Someone who *doesn't like you.*"

"You're bluffing!" Emily yelled. But Mariella ignored her and looked closely at the newspaper. "Is that the same boy you've drawn over and over and over again in your sketchbook?" she asked me.

"M-my . . . sketchbook?" I stammered. "I . . . I told you not to look at my sketchbook!" I felt my cheeks growing red.

"Oh, I looked at it, all right," Mariella said. "All your dumb drawings."

"Hey, they're not dumb!" Emily said.

"Do you have a *crush*?" Mariella taunted, pointing to the picture of Orlando in the box. "I noticed you even drew pictures of my *dad*—ew! Jillian likes my dad! Or who's that other stupid guy you drew, way in the back of the book? Maybe you like him! He looks totally *old*!"

Tears sprang to my eyes.

"Come on!" I said to Emily. I pulled her across the street, back into the building. Montego buzzed us right in.

I crawled into bed, feeling angrier than I'd ever been. Mariella was spying on me, and she was looking through my sketchbook. My *private* sketchbook. At those pictures of my *dad*. God, I'd written a little poem next to one of the drawings too, about how much I missed him. Had Mariella read it and laughed? My insides felt all knotted up. How could she not understand? Why did she have to be so *mean*?

And then I saw it, on her bedside table. Her cell phone. I could erase all the numbers in her phone book. She deserves it, I thought.

I picked it up and flipped it open. It glowed a soft green. There was the phone book button. I bet there was an easy way to erase it all at once.

I held the phone in my hands for a long time. But for some reason, I couldn't do it. It just seemed . . . too terrible. I closed the phone and put it back. I stared at it for a long time, willing myself to pick it up again. But hasn't she been nothing but terrible to you since you met her? I asked myself. Still, I just couldn't.

Frustrated, I put my pillow over my head. A few minutes later, Mariella came back inside, but I pretended to be asleep.

James Killian's
School picture
(from TV)

I didn't sleep a wink that night. How could I? I wanted to call the police, but I didn't want Mariella to hear me. I tossed and turned, and tossed and turned. What could I do? How could I help Orlando?

When I got out of bed the next morning, the kidnapping was all over the TV news and the papers. The picture of the kidnapped boy, the boy I'd drawn over and over in my sketchbook, was plastered on the cover of the *New York Post*, as well as on NY1. The boy's real name was James Killian.

"The Killian family lives in an affluent neighborhood in Westchester County," the newscaster said, speaking in front of the tall glowing billboards in Times Square. "James attends high school at Westchester Academy but has been on summer vacation. Friends and neighbors say he comes into Manhattan quite often."

A teenage boy came on the screen. "James used to go down to Canal Street, to Pearl Paint to buy silk-screen stuff there."

Despite how freaked out I was, my heart did a tiny flip. The boy *was* into art!

The newswoman came on again. "Two Saturdays ago, sources say that James went into Manhattan to do exactly that—buy art supplies. But he never returned home. Witnesses say they saw a boy who looked like James the morning he went missing. And one woman, Angela Barrett of Kips Bay, says she saw the boy talking to a man later that evening. The police sketch artists drew up this composite."

The drawing on the screen was of a long-faced, scowling man. He looks familiar, I thought. But I couldn't figure out from where. I tried to remember everyone I'd seen on the elevators in the Dakota, at camp, or on the street, but I couldn't place him.

I had gotten up before Mariella, but I felt her eyes on my back as soon as she walked into the kitchen. I took a big gulp of milk.

My mom switched the channel, but the newscasters seemed to be talking about the kidnapping on every station.

"Fifteen-year-old James Killian is from a wealthy and respected family," a newscaster went on. "His mother,

Katherine, is an orthopedic surgeon at Westchester Hospital, and his father, Senator Allen Killian, has been an influential New York State senator for over ten years."

"Poor Senator Killian!" my mother gasped. "I interviewed him for the magazine not that long ago!"

Whoa, I thought. My mom had talked to the cute boy's *dad*?

The newscaster paused for a moment and shuffled some papers. "Since James's disappearance, the family has received several threatening letters. We'll now go to Andrew Martin, NYPD bureau chief, who has some words on this."

The news switched to a man in a New York City police uniform. "In both a ransom note and a phone call, the kidnapper has asked again for a ransom of one million dollars."

My mother gasped.

"One million dollars isn't that much," Mariella scoffed. "You can't even buy a good apartment for one million dollars."

"Yes it is!" I hissed. What planet was she on?

The camera cut to a small girl in pigtails. "I'm James's sister," she said. She looked about eight or nine. "Please return my brother."

His mom got on next: "Please, please bring back our son," she said. "He is a sweet boy, and we love him very much. We are all very upset, and . . ." She put her hand over the camera, obviously too choked up to talk.

"Is anyone *looking* for him?" I said. "The police? They didn't say anything about that."

"I'm sure the police are looking for him," my mother

explained. "But they don't want to give the kidnapper that impression. They are trying, I think, to show him the emotional side of things, and how upset his family is, in hopes that the kidnapper will come to his senses and return the boy unharmed."

"I saw the police do that in a movie once," Mariella murmured.

Mariella and my mother watched the television silently. They had no idea that the kidnapper and James were hiding *right across the street.* I was ready to blurt it out. *I know where he is!* I started chewing frantically on my fingernails.

Another sketch of the suspected kidnapper flashed on the screen.

"That guy looks familiar," my mother said. "Where do I know him from?"

As the news continued, I was getting more and more nervous. I thought about poor adorable Orlando—er, James—starving to death. I had to tell my mother, but I couldn't. There was no way. If I did, I'd have to admit I'd ditched camp. I wouldn't just get a babysitter; she'd kill me. And besides, we'd been spying on James. What if we got hauled off to jail ourselves?

But I didn't want James to get hurt, or worse.

I could feel Mariella staring at me. "You seem awfully interested in that case," she said in a smart-alecky tone. She was painting her nails between bites of toast.

"Well, I—I—" I stammered.

"It's almost time for you to go to camp," my mother interrupted, looking worried. "This kidnapping stuff has made me really concerned. Is there enough supervision at your camp? Maybe I should go down and wait for the bus with you," she said, biting her lip.

"Come on, Mom," I said, trying to sound as normal as possible. "I'll be fine."

"No," my mom said, shaking her head. "This is serious, Jillian. You're only eleven. Maybe I'm letting you have too much freedom here. That boy was fifteen!"

"But . . . but don't you have to get to work?"

Mariella was grinning maniacally.

"I can be a little late," my mother said. "Come on. Get your stuff. You're going to miss the bus if you sit here any longer."

"All right," I said. My mind was racing. I would actually have to *go* to camp today?

But there was nothing I could do. She ushered me into the elevator, then out into the courtyard and onto the street. I gazed up at the apartment building across the street, looking for poor James's window. As soon as I got home from camp, I was definitely going to call the police.

"What's the matter?" my mother said, putting her hand on my shoulder.

"Nothing," I muttered.

"You know, Jillian, I really appreciate your cooperation over the last few weeks," she said softly. "I know it's been hard. But you've really made the best of it. It means quite a lot to me. And I think, in time, you and Mariella will become friends."

I snorted. Fat chance of that happening.

"You know Dad always told you to . . . oh . . . what was that phrase they used in *The Lion King*? It meant don't worry . . ."

"*Hakuna matata*," I mumbled. I hadn't said it in a long time.

"That's right!" my mother said happily. "Remember how much you guys used to love that movie? You always watched it together."

"Yeah," I said. "That and *Lilo & Stitch* and *Shrek*. I think Dad liked cartoons more than I did. Remember he used to sing all the songs in the shower?"

"Yeah," my mother said, a little sadly. "And remember he used to play with all your little rubber duckies and boats?"

"He was so silly." I smiled.

"I really miss him," my mom said.

My eyes widened—I'd thought she'd forgotten about him. "So do I."

This felt like such a perfect moment to tell my mom about James. I wanted to so badly, I thought I'd burst. She was standing right here. I could open my mouth and say something—and then *she* could call the police. But I felt paralyzed.

The bus was turning the corner onto Seventy-second Street. My mother squeezed my hand. I sighed heavily.

The bus stopped at the curb, and the door hissed open. "Hi!" Fred said happily. "How's my favorite camper?"

And then, another voice. "Jillian, so nice to see you!"

It was Rainbow. My worst fears were confirmed. She

craned her neck around the front seat and smiled down at me.

"Well, you certainly are well versed in the art world!" Rainbow exclaimed to my mom. "When Jillian told me that you were going to the Dia, I was really impressed!"

"The Dia?" my mother said, looking at me questioningly.

"Um . . . ," I said, flustered. I knew I had to get out of this situation—and *fast.* I walked up to Fred's hairy ear and hissed, "This is life or death. Please close the door."

He looked up at me. There must have been extreme urgency in my face. Fred reached for the release that pulled the door shut. "Aye, aye, Captain," he said, and winked.

The doors closed creakily in my mother's face. Her mouth opened in surprise. I gave her a what-can-you-do, he's-a-crazy-old-bus-driver shrug and waved goodbye. She stepped away from the curb, a little perplexed, but then, not knowing what else to do, waved goodbye back. I gave my new friend Fred a little squeeze on the shoulder and found a seat.

strange
sketchy
hair!

Sketch of
possible kidnapper

At the end of the day, the camp bus let me off in front of my building. The day hadn't been that bad. It was drizzly, so we didn't have to go to the park. Instead, we played dodgeball on Barnard and Columbia's indoor basketball courts. Hurling spongy balls at the younger kids got rid of a lot of my frustration. Even Rainbow commented on how well I'd participated today.

I headed straight up to Mrs. W's apartment. "Mipsy," I murmured. "Mipsy-Wipsy!" The cat purred and rubbed up against my side. I picked up her paws and we danced together for a few seconds. But then, distracted, I quickly moved to the window. James. He was still there, lying on his bed, barely moving. I ran to the phone and called Emily's apartment. I got her family's voice mail. I hung up feeling jittery. At least James wasn't dead. Every once in a while, I saw his hand twitch.

But James's family was receiving ransom notes. The kidnapper meant business.

If only Emily and I could get inside that apartment. Maybe we could figure out a way to rescue James without the kidnapper knowing what we were up to.

I flipped on NY1 to see if there had been any breaks in the case. But there was nothing new, just the same videos of Senator Killian and his family, and pictures of a more clean-cut James.

The police sketch of the kidnapper flickered back up on the screen. I stared at it. There was something about the nose . . . and the eyes. . . .

I grabbed my sketchbook out of my bag and flipped to a blank page. I drew the sketch off the TV quickly, getting the essence of the eyes and the nose. I filled in the chin and the forehead, and then the hair. Hmm. I added a mustache. And a little beard, a key around the neck, and glasses.

Interesting.

Finally, I added a tall white hat—that said KAPUTSA'S.

"Oh my god," I said quietly to myself. "It's him!"

The kidnapper looked exactly like Jacques, the angry cheese guy from Kaputsa's.

"Could it be?" I whispered. Then I remembered the bad photo of Mariella we'd found at the Christmas party. Hadn't he . . . hadn't he been in those, too? I ran to Mrs. W's drawer and frantically riffled through the photos until I found the one of him. There he was, in a sweater-vest, holding a tall glass. He wrinkled his face snootily, as if he'd gotten a whiff of bad-smelling cheese. I gasped. It was definitely him. I was sure of it.

I called Emily, but there was still no answer. I fed Mipsy and went back down to my own apartment to try Emily again. Finally, she answered. "What happened to you?" she whispered. "I waited at Mrs. W's door for a long time."

"I had to go to camp," I said quickly. "But that's not important. I had a huge breakthrough."

"A breakthrough? On what?"

I looked around. Mariella was in the other room, watching a *Friends* rerun. I didn't know if she was listening, but I didn't want to risk it. "Meet me in the courtyard," I said. "Five minutes."

Downstairs, I showed Emily the drawing I'd done. "This was from the sketch on TV," I explained. "Look like anyone familiar?"

"Kaputsa's . . . ," Emily whispered. Then she looked up at me, her mouth wide open. "The *Kaputsa's cheese guy*?"

"Doesn't it look like him?" I asked. I pulled out Mrs. W's picture. "Look! Here he is again! And didn't you say this party was for tenants of this building, but it took place across the street?"

"Yeah . . . ," Emily said. "It did. . . ."

"So we know Jacques has been inside the building," I explained. "Isn't it possible that he lives there?"

"Well, I guess . . . ," Emily said. She looked back and forth from the photo to the sketch in disbelief. Then she looked at me. "What do we do?" she whispered.

"I think we should call the police," I said.

"Maybe you're right," Emily breathed in relief. "We could make an anonymous tip. If we don't tell them who we are, they won't be able to tell our parents."

We decided to make the call from Mrs. W's. Emily picked up one cordless phone and I got on the extension. But the police station phone rang and rang and rang.

Finally, someone picked up. "Twentieth Precinct," a man's gruff voice said.

"Um, hi," I said, clearing my throat, trying to sound a little bit older. "I have some information on the James Killian kidnapping?"

"You do? Hold on a sec. . . ." We heard him shuffling papers. "Okay. Go ahead?"

"Well, um, I think I know where James Killian is."

"Okay . . ."

I told him the address. "And . . . I don't know the apartment, but it's the fourth window from the right . . ."

"I don't understand," the policeman said. "You don't know the apartment, you just know the window?"

"I—"

"We saw him through our window, from across Seventy-second Street," Emily interrupted.

Another pause. "How old are you girls, anyway?" the

officer finally said. "We don't mess around here, so if this is a joke . . ."

"No, it's not a joke!" I said. "We're *positive* it's James Killian! We've been watching him from my friend's apartment for days! I'm cat-sitting for her, and we saw him through the binoculars—" I got a sharp kick from Emily. *Binoculars,* she mouthed. We weren't sure if spying on people was illegal.

But the policeman completely ignored that and pressed on. "So, let me get this straight. You've seen somebody through the window who looks like Senator Killian's son, but you've only seen him through binoculars?"

"Yeah . . . ," I said slowly.

"Through a dirty, possibly blurry window. Is that right?"

I exchanged a look with Emily. Could it be possible? Maybe the boy across the street wasn't James at all. Maybe our eyes and imaginations had been playing tricks on us and we just *wanted* it to be the kidnapped boy. I stared at the window again. The policeman was right—James's window *was* pretty smudged.

"Is there any way you can check it out?" I said in a small voice.

He sighed. "Well, to get into that apartment, we'd need more evidence. We can't get a search warrant on a tip about something somebody's seen from a window across the street. But how about this—I'll send a patrol car around. I'll have somebody check out the building." He didn't sound very convincing at all.

We hung up and stared at each other. I felt like all the air had seeped out of me.

"Maybe it *isn't* James," Emily said quietly.

"But it looks like him," I said, pressing my nose against the window. I hadn't even mentioned my suspicions about the Cheese Man. Then again, if they didn't believe us about seeing James through a window, they wouldn't buy that I'd figured out the kidnapper's identity by adding a beard, glasses, and hat to the sketch.

"This is so frustrating!" Emily said, kicking one of Mipsy's toys as we left the apartment. "We just told the police what we know, and they're not going to do a thing! Time's running out!"

I thought for a minute, staring at the numbers in the elevator. "You know what, that *is* James over there. I'm sure of it. But . . . but maybe we should rescue him ourselves. We already know where he is, and we wouldn't arrive with a police car and sirens. We just have to get to the right apartment and break in somehow. Jacques totally wouldn't suspect us, because we're kids."

"But it's too dangerous!" Emily argued. "Hello, Bulldog?"

"I don't know," I said. "But we have to figure out a way!" I headed for the courtyard. "Why didn't Bulldog see James come into the building? Wouldn't he have noticed?"

Emily thought for a moment. "The news says James was kidnapped three weeks ago on a Saturday. The Yankees were playing the Red Sox that evening. I remember 'cause my parents were having a big fight over the game. Maybe Bulldog was glued to his TV or radio and wasn't paying attention."

"I wish the Yankees were playing Boston *now*," I said. "If that's the case, we could sneak right past him!"

"Jillian?" a voice called.

I turned around. There was my mother, bag slung over her shoulder, just returning from work. I quickly shoved the picture of Jacques into my sketchbook.

"Hi, Mom," I said.

"Hi, Mrs. Fairley," Emily said. She'd met my mom once by the elevators.

"Jillian, you'd better come upstairs and get ready for Mariella's tae kwon do demonstration," my mom said.

I wrinkled my nose. "Do I have to go?"

My mother sighed, exasperated. "Yes. You do. Now, come on."

"We'll talk tomorrow," I mouthed to Emily as I walked away.

"What about camp?" she mouthed back.

"I'm gonna ditch," I mouthed, and nodded. I pointed my thumb in the air, gesturing that I'd meet her at Mrs. W's at our normal time the next morning. I was going to ditch out of camp even if it meant my mother would find out that I'd been bagging for the whole summer.

Even if it meant a *babysitter.*

James's life depended on it.

Mariella's
mom
(when she was 14)

The other members of Mariella's exclusive tae kwon do dojo were all about sixty-five years old. They stood in a large circle in shorts pulled up too high and black socks, with Coke-bottle glasses and wrinkly faces. *These* are the people she beats up every week? Well, no wonder she's the best in her class!

But then when the demonstration started, I was actually pretty surprised. Even the guy who looked like he was about two hundred years old was super-strong. The thrill of the night was watching an old lady pick Mariella up over her head and throw her down onto the mats. Out of the corner of my eye, I saw my mother and Michael wince.

But still, I couldn't totally enjoy it. My mind spun, trying to come up with a plan for what we should do about James. I wondered how we could get past Bulldog. Maybe we could bribe him with egg sandwiches and sushi? After all, that was how I'd become friends with Montego. But Bulldog didn't look like the egg sandwich or sushi type. He looked like he probably ate lots of steak. Raw.

And then something else occurred to me: even if we did get into the building, there was no way we could get into the actual *apartment*. It wasn't as if we could knock on the door and the Cheese Man—if he *was* the kidnapper— would just let us in.

I sighed. Now Mariella was in the center of the room, all by herself. The sensei was making jerky movements with his hands. Michael leaned down to me. "This is where she does her famous Flying Snake move," he said proudly. "She's the only one in the class who can do it."

Well, duh, I thought. It sounds perfect for her because her face is so reptilian.

Mariella spun around and did a couple of backflips, then a series of punches, and then somehow jumped into the air and stretched her body out flat. Right before she hit the ground, she coiled into a neat forward roll.

When she finished, everyone clapped politely. My mother clapped more loudly than anyone else.

"This calls for a treat," Michael said when the exhibition was over. "Tasti D-Lite?"

"Yum," Mariella smiled sweetly. "And it's nonfat, perfect for my diet!"

I snorted.

When we got to the shop, I ordered a small cup of Butterfinger and wandered outside. Butterfinger was my favorite flavor, but I couldn't eat it. My stomach was clenched and my mind just kept going in circles. I knew I had to do something fast. I didn't know what that something would be. But if I *didn't* do something, or if I did the wrong thing, James would die. I was sure of it.

I let some of the ice cream slide off the spoon and back into the bowl.

"Problem?" Mariella stood next to me.

"No," I shot back.

"Guilty conscience, maybe?" she asked nastily. "Are you thinking about that kidnapped boy? How do you know him?"

I didn't answer.

"Or are you thinking about that stupid older guy that you drew in your sketchbook? Who is that? Is that your *dad*?"

I had had just about enough of her. "It *is* my dad, as a matter of fact!" I exploded. "How dare you make fun of him! You don't know anything about him! You wouldn't even understand what it's like to miss somebody like I miss him!" Even as I said it, I knew it wasn't true. But I was just so mad, I couldn't control myself.

She gave me a look that could have stopped the Seventy-second Street traffic dead.

"You don't know what you're *talking* about!" she said. "You think I don't miss my mom? Every day?"

"Is that what you *cry* about on the phone?"

As I was saying it, I knew it was mean. And Mariella's face crumpled. She looked for a moment like she was going to start sobbing. But then her eyes narrowed. Her nostrils flared. Her face grew beet red. She threw her cone on the ground. It splattered, cone side up, on the sidewalk. "I hate you," she growled. She reached down, scooped a handful of ice cream up off the sidewalk, and flung it in my face. A big clump of it landed in my hair.

I took a scoop of my ice cream on my spoon and fired it at her. It landed right in the middle of her stupid shirt. *Splat.*

"My Diane von Furstenberg top!" she squealed, quickly fanning her shirt away from her body. Steam practically puffed out of her nose. "I'll flip you, I swear," she said. "I'll do my Flying Snake move on you so fast, your head will spin."

"Try me!" I roared. She ran toward me and I backed up. And then she ran past me and I chased her.

Suddenly we were on the ground. Rolling, pulling hair, squealing. I was so mad, I couldn't see straight. But Mariella was stronger than I was. She got on top of me and held down my hands. I struggled, but she wouldn't budge.

"Get off me," I roared.

"Baby," she said, sneering. "Go home to wherever you came from."

"What's going on here?" my mother shouted.

I looked up.

Michael and my mom were standing over us, looking shocked.

I squirmed out from underneath her and finally managed to stand. Mariella and I were both crying.

"Honestly, girls," my mother continued, shaking her head. Her lower lip wobbled. Uh-oh, I thought. My mom's gonna start crying. "When I didn't see you out front, my first thought was that something terrible had happened."

"We weren't kidnapped, if that's what you were worried about," Mariella said in a small voice. "New York isn't *that* dangerous."

"You never know!" my mother said. And then she *did* start crying. "They're probably never going to find that poor kidnapped boy. And what if you girls got kidnapped and they never found *you*? I wouldn't be able to live!"

"Come now," Michael said, putting his arm around her shoulder. "It's okay."

But suddenly, with all this talk about kidnapping, I just lost it. I blurted: "Mom, I know where the kidnapped boy is—he's in the building across the street and they've locked him in a room and he'll be okay but somebody's got to save him!"

The words came out all in a jumble. There were tears rolling down my face and my nose was dripping. I let out a big sniff. My mother was silent. A big drip from her cone plopped onto her shoe.

And then she wiped a tear from her cheek and smiled. "Honey," she said. "You know that's not true."

I sputtered, "Not true? But . . . but it *is* true!"

"You've had an exciting couple of weeks," my mother said, sniffing and giving me a small concerned smile. "I

135

know you've been under a lot of stress. We all have. And that story, on TV now . . . I can see how that might worry you, being new to the city. . . ."

"But . . . ," I said desperately.

"The police have it under control," Michael said in a kind voice. "There's nothing any of us can do."

I looked back and forth from Michael to my mother in shock. They didn't believe me. They just thought I was some stupid kid who was letting her imagination run wild. They weren't even *listening* to me.

"Now, what's going on between you two girls?" my mother said sternly, recovering.

"Nothing," I muttered.

Surprisingly, Mariella didn't say anything either.

"Nothing?" Michael asked. "Look, girls, what you're feeling is understandable. There have been many changes for both of you. Jillian, you had to move. And Mariella, you have to share your room. It's hard. But fighting isn't going to get you anywhere."

Out of the corner of my eye, I saw Mariella roll her eyes.

"Don't roll your eyes at your father!" my mother said to her.

My mouth dropped open. Was my mother actually *disciplining* Mariella?

"We're going home," my mom said. "And you girls are going to spend some time in your room together."

"I don't have to listen to you!" Mariella screamed. She turned and started storming off down Seventy-second.

"Get back here," Michael said, running after her. "You *will* listen to her. Another crack like that out of you, and you'll be punished for more than just one night. Now, come on. This way." He grabbed her shoulder and pointed her in the direction of the Dakota.

o o o

For the first hour alone in our room, we didn't speak to each other. Mariella played games on her cell phone, and I stared out the window.

Then, out of the blue, Mariella said, "I hate my dad."

"I hate my mom," I said reluctantly.

"I hate them both," Mariella said angrily.

"I do too," I said.

We didn't say anything else for a while. And then I heard a sniffling sound coming from Mariella's half of the room. I looked at her and saw her wipe something off her face. Tears. Suddenly my throat felt kind of tight.

"Hey, you okay?" I said. My voice sounded weird.

Mariella sighed. "I'm sorry I said that thing about your dad looking stupid. He doesn't."

I looked down at my bedspread. "Whatever," I said. "I'm sorry I said that thing about your crying on the phone."

"It *is* my mom that I cry about, though," she added. "I really miss her." Mariella looked me in the eye. She wasn't crying anymore, but she sounded so sad. And I knew exactly how she felt.

"I know what you mean," I said. "I miss my dad, too."

"When did he die?"

"Two and a half years ago."

"My mom died a year and a half ago. When I was eleven. Your age."

We didn't say anything again for a while.

137

"My mom used to use this really great bubble bath that she got in France," Mariella said, finally. "I tried to find it when I was in Switzerland, but I couldn't. This is a picture of her." She handed me a framed picture from her nightstand.

"She was pretty," I murmured. She looked like an older version of Mariella.

"Sometimes when I think about her, it feels like getting punched in the stomach," Mariella said.

"Same here," I agreed. "I hope wherever my dad is now, he knows how much I love him and miss him."

"I bet he does," Mariella said.

"Sometimes when it gets really bad, I draw pictures for my dad. My dad really liked my pictures. He had them hanging up at his office."

Mariella nodded. "I do tae kwon do because my mom practiced it. I think about her a lot when I'm doing my Flying Snake."

I had to hold back a giggle when I thought about Mariella and her Flying Snake.

"That's why I didn't go to the wedding," Mariella continued, playing with a loose thread on her bedspread. "My dad bought me a plane ticket and everything, but I just . . . I didn't want to see my dad marrying somebody else. I went to the airport, but I didn't get on the plane. I couldn't do it. My dad was really upset. I think your mom's mad at me too."

"It was a nice wedding, I guess," I said quietly.

Ramsay made a little yip. I jumped back. "C'mere,

Ramsay," Mariella said, leaning down. The dog climbed into her arms.

"He's a good dog," she said. "If you get to know him." She held him out and motioned for me to hold him. I shook my head. Mariella looked hurt. "You really don't like Ramsay, huh?"

"It's not that," I said. "It's more like . . . I'm kinda scared of dogs. Even little ones." As soon as the words were out of my mouth, I felt a little nervous. A couple of hours before, we were beating each other up on the sidewalk, and here I was, confessing to her one of my biggest secrets.

"Really?" Mariella said.

"Don't laugh!" I said.

But she wasn't laughing. She was just looking at me and nodding.

"My dad was afraid of them too," I said.

Mariella put her hand to her lips, thinking. "It's okay. I guess I won't make fun of you." she paused. "Not *too* much, anyway." I looked up and she gave me a little smirk. "The thing about most dogs is you just need to show them that you're not afraid of them. If you act tough enough, you can fool almost anyone."

We fell into silence again. I watched the cabs drift up the street.

"So, do you really know that kidnapped boy?" Mariella asked.

I shrugged.

"I saw those drawings you did of that kid before the story came out. What do you know?"

I didn't know if I could trust her. Even though we'd just admitted a bunch of stuff to each other, I wasn't sure. "You've been kinda mean to me . . ."

"I know. But . . . I don't want us to be mean to each other anymore. I'm really serious."

"Are you gonna tell my mom about camp?" I said in a small voice.

"So you *are* ditching!" Mariella said, clapping her hands. "I knew it!"

"I—" I started.

"No, no, it's no big deal. I can't believe you're brave enough to ditch! But I won't tell. I promise. Besides, you saw me downstairs that one night with Jason. *Surely* you've heard me talking about him on the phone. My dad *hates* that I'm into boys. So you could tell on me about that, right?"

"Hrmph," I said. "I guess . . ."

Mariella was quiet for a while.

"Look," she said finally. "If you tell me, maybe I can help."

I thought about it. Emily and I had kind of run out of options. Time was running out. And I didn't know what else to do. So I told her. I told her how I knew about the kidnapped boy. It was a long story, but it felt good to get it all out.

After I finished, Mariella was quiet. I stared up at the glow-in-the-dark stars on our ceiling. I bit my bottom lip.

But then she spoke. "That is the coolest thing I have ever heard."

"You mean it?" I said. "You believe me?"

"Absolutely." Her voice sounded all breathy and excited.

"And you know what? I think I might know a way to get into the building. *And* into the Cheese Man's apartment."

"Really?" I said. "How?"

"I'm kind of tired," Mariella said, yawning. "We wouldn't be able to do it until tomorrow, anyway."

"*How?*" I repeated.

"I'll tell you in the morning," she said, sounding like the same old Mariella. "I have to make some calls first." And then she turned her back toward me and started dialing her phone.

I really hoped this wasn't just one of her tricks.

FRED

17

The next day, I woke up to the sun streaming through the window. I sprang out of bed, got dressed quickly, and dashed down to meet the camp bus. I was all out of museums that I could lie about, and was prepared to just tell Rainbow the truth: I had to take care of a private matter, and I'd explain it tomorrow. I didn't care if my mom punished me. This was way more important.

Fred rolled the bus up to the curb and opened the door. "She isn't on the bus today," he said, clearly meaning Rainbow.

"Oh," I said. I was so prepared for Rainbow to be on the bus that I didn't have a backup plan if she *wasn't.* "C-can you . . ." I stammered. "Can you, um . . ."

"I'm gonna tell her you're sick," Fred said, winking at me. "Right?"

"Yeah," I said.

"A terrible flu," he continued. "Too sick to come to camp."

"Right," I said. I smiled. "Thanks a lot, Fred." I stepped away from the bus.

"What's *she* doing here?" Emily said when Mariella and I met her at Mrs. W's.

"She knows a way to get into James's building," I explained.

Emily's mouth opened. "You told *her* about James? Are you crazy?"

"Yeah," I said hurriedly. "But see, Mariella knows how we can get into the building *and* into the Cheese Man's apartment. . . ."

"I want to see this James first," Mariella said. "At the window."

"Fine," I said, exasperated. I led her to the window and handed her the binoculars. James sat perfectly still, staring at the wall. He looked exhausted. Mariella studied him closely.

"Amazing," she murmured.

"Okay, spill it," I said after a few seconds.

She put the binoculars down, paused dramatically, and then said in a haughty tone, "Jason can get us inside. And I think I know where the Cheese Man keeps a spare key."

"Jason?" I said. "Spare key?"

"You know who Jason is," Mariella growled, making a face. "But Jason is part two of the plan. First, we have to get the Cheese Man's house key. Jillian, I think you're right: I think the kidnapper *is* the Cheese Man. When I called Jason this morning, he said that yeah, a weird guy who works at Kaputsa's lived in the building. Apparently he inherited a duplex from a rich uncle."

"Well, I *knew* I was right," I said. "The police sketch looked just like him."

"But what's that you said about a house key?" Emily asked.

I thought for a second. "Is that the key he wears around his neck?"

"It's *one* of the keys," Mariella explained. "I have a friend whose older brother works in the produce department at Kaputsa's. I asked him if he knew anything about the Cheese Man. Everyone who works there thinks the cheese guy is a big weirdo. He said the Cheese Man has all kinds of strange habits, like, y'know, talking to the cheese when he's slicing it, and sharpening his knife for exactly three minutes every morning. And he's so particular about his cheese slicing that he won't even keep anything in his pockets or his apron, as it might throw him 'off balance,' whatever that means."

"What *does* it mean?" I asked.

"Yeah," said Emily. "Get to the point, please."

"What that *means* is that while he's working, he keeps his keys—and, oh yeah, he has keys not only to his house but to his 'private humidor of cheese'—not in his apron or his pocket like a regular person, but on a hook behind the counter." Mariella stopped and smiled, looking very pleased with herself.

"*Really?*" Emily said.

I suddenly remembered the first time I saw him, holding his big key chain, reminding me of a jailer. But still, this new information didn't really help us very much.

"Yeah, it'll be *real* easy to get the keys," I said sarcastically. "How are we going to get behind the counter?"

"We go to Kaputsa's and wait for him to hang up his keys and start slicing," Mariella said simply.

"How do you propose we do that?" I asked.

"Well, we'll go there, and I'll pretend like I'm really interested in cheese," Mariella said. "And while I'm distracting him, you'll slip behind the counter and grab his keys!"

"Why do *I* have to get the keys?" I said. "That's the hard part!"

"You're smaller than I am!" Mariella reasoned. "You're less noticeable!"

"Well, that's where you're wrong," I said. "The Cheese Man has it in for me. I caused a huge disaster at the Kaputsa's cheese counter! He told me never to come to his section again!"

"I was there!" Emily said, nodding.

Mariella thought for a moment. "Maybe we could disguise you?"

"Actually . . ." I trailed off. I had an idea. I walked back into Mrs. W's bedroom and found the coconut cake hat and big sunglasses. I tried them on and looked at myself in the mirror. I definitely didn't look like Jillian Fairley, the girl who had caused a ruckus at Kaputsa's cheese counter.

I walked out in the disguise. "Does this work?" I asked them.

They both looked at me for a moment. "It's perfect," Mariella said.

Emily nodded. "You may look a little weird," she said slowly. "But you definitely don't look like you."

"It's set, then," Mariella said. "We'd better go over to Kaputsa's now, before the lunch crowd comes."

"Now?" I said.

"Of course," Mariella said. "We can't waste any time. Ready?"

I swallowed hard. "I guess," I said.

But I wasn't so sure.

The Cheese Man's
keys

The three of us stood in front of Kaputsa's, working up the courage to go inside.

"Ready?" Mariella asked. She was wearing a huge bright pink feathered hat that belonged to Mrs. W so she would be even more noticeable.

"Yes," I said, adjusting my own Mrs. W hat. The glasses kept sliding down my nose. I pushed them back up. My heart thumped in my chest.

"He's slicing now! I can see keys on the peg behind the

counter," Emily said, squinting through the window. "Jillian, you'll have to sneak behind the counter from the far end, walk the whole way to the other side, and grab them."

"That seems impossible!" I said. "Can't I just reach around from the other side of the counter?"

"It doesn't look like it," Emily said. "The space behind the counter looks too wide. You'll just have to slide in behind it. Really quickly."

"Come on," Mariella said, grabbing my sleeve. "It's now or never."

Emily gave me a scared look. "You don't have to do this, you know. I mean, maybe we could try to find another way."

"It'll be okay," I said. "Think of James." I crossed my fingers.

"You're right," Emily said uneasily. "Good luck!"

I hadn't been to Kaputsa's since the day I caused the disaster. The closer we got to the cheese counter, the stronger the smell got. We crouched behind a giant pickle barrel and planned our strategy.

"There are the keys," Mariella whispered. I spotted them. Emily was right: the area behind the counter had only one opening, near a bunch of olive barrels. I would have to get behind the counter there, then walk the whole way to the other side, grab the keys, and walk the whole way back.

"I'll get him out from behind the counter," Mariella said. "You pretend to be browsing around at the olives. Once he comes out, make a run for it!"

"I don't know if I can do this," I said, my voice shaking.

"You can do it," Mariella said, squeezing my arm. "Trust me. If you can ditch out of camp without your mom finding out, you can get past this stupid Cheese Man."

But . . . he's the kidnapper, I wanted to scream. Instead I just nodded.

Mariella stepped out from behind the pickle barrel and stood in line at the cheese counter. She looked back at me and frowned when she saw me still crouched down behind her. "Go look at the olives!" she mouthed angrily.

I moved slowly toward the olive barrels. The Cheese Man glanced in my direction. My heart stopped: did he recognize me, even in the hat and glasses?

He gave me a long look, then went back to slicing cheese for a customer.

"Next!" the Cheese Man roared when he was done.

"Hello!" Mariella squealed brightly. "How are you today?"

The Cheese Man grunted.

"I'm looking for something with the consistency of Velveeta," Mariella said. "Do you have cheese like that?"

The Cheese Man stuck his bottom lip out and sniffed. "Of course not!" he said in his snooty French accent. "If you want something like that, go to a bodega! Not Kaputsa's cheese counter!"

"So you don't have anything like that behind the counter?" Mariella said in a sweet but firm voice. It was the kind of voice she used with Michael when she was trying to get her way.

"No!" Jacques said, raising his voice even higher.

I crouched behind the olive barrels. What was she doing? It wasn't working.

Mariella looked around at the tables of cheese. "What about this kind of cheese?" she asked, picking up a block.

"That's parmigiano," the Cheese Man said.

"Oh, yummy! I love parmigiano!" Mariella said, stumbling over the word. "Can I just eat it whole, like this?" She put the whole block up to her wide-open mouth.

"No!" Jacques said, frustrated. "That kind of serious cheese eating is only for the very advanced cheese connoisseur. Your palate is not refined enough!"

"Oh," Mariella said, looking at the other tables. "Can you show me a cheese that I *could* appreciate?"

"Well, there's that one," Jacques said, pointing. "Gouda. That is very good."

"Gouda," Mariella said. She walked to another table of cheese, one that was farther from the counter. "How about this kind of cheese? Farmhouse cheddar, it says. Is this kind good?"

"Haven't you heard of *cheddar*?" the Cheese Man said, rolling his eyes. "Do you need something from behind the counter? Otherwise, you can help yourself."

"Oh, but you're the expert!" Mariella said. "Will you help me choose the perfect block of cheddar?"

The Cheese Man did a snotty little shake of his head. "They are all the same cheese," he said, exasperated. "All of them are excellent. What does it matter which block you choose?"

"*Please?*" Mariella said. She squinted at his nametag. "Please . . . Jacques? That's *such* a nice name. Is it French? I want the most *perfect* block of cheddar, and I bet you could find it for me!"

Jacques paused for a moment, furrowing his brow. I huddled by the olives. He was going to say no. He was going to tell Mariella to get out of his cheese section.

But to my surprise, after a few moments, Jacques shook his head and sucked his teeth. "Fine," he said gruffly. "If after that, you will go away and leave this department to the serious cheese connoisseurs."

And he walked out from behind the counter and over to Mariella.

Mariella's eyes widened and met mine. "Go!" she whispered.

Ducking down, I dashed behind the counter, trying not to slide on the pieces of mashed cheese on the ground.

The Cheese Man turned back to check on his counter. Luckily, I ducked just in time, but I was now nose to nose with a whole bunch of slabs of putrid, rancid cheese.

I felt like I was going to throw up.

You can do all the throwing up you want once you're back out on the sidewalk, I told myself. I held my nose securely. The Cheese Man turned back to Mariella, and I reached up for his keys. But they slipped out of my hands and fell . . . into a large open bucket of crumbled blue cheese that was sitting on the floor!

"Eep!" I said. The keys had disappeared into the goo. "Guhh," I said, getting a whiff. I held my breath and plunged my hand into the bucket. The cheese felt gooey and cold. I rooted around for a while, making a huge mess.

"No, I don't know, maybe *this* block?" I heard Mariella

say. "Don't you think this block is maybe a better *shape* than the other one? But then again, this one is so *orange*..."

"You're wasting my time!" the Cheese Man said.

Aha! *There* they were! I dug out the keys. They were covered in goo, and so was my arm. I shoved them in my pocket anyway, and made a dash for the exit.

"Hey!" a voice boomed.

I looked up. The Cheese Man had turned around and was coming back to the counter. "Are you stealing cheese back there, young lady?" he demanded.

He scampered back to the counter, blocking me in. "Why is your hand covered in blue cheese?" he roared. "You're a thief!"

I was trapped. I looked right and left. Mariella stood at the other side of the counter. The only way I could get around him would be to climb up onto the counter and slide down the other side. The Cheese Man was striding toward me angrily. Mariella stretched her arms out to help me.

I boosted myself up onto the counter, flipped over the side awkwardly, and slid down the glass front. The Cheese Man screamed. "What are you *doing*?"

Mariella caught me on the other side. My blue cheese–covered hand had messed up her shirt, but she didn't care. "Good work!" she said. She held my hand and we made a break for it.

"Come back here!" the Cheese Man said. "Thief!"

We could see the exit in front of us. A few checkout clerks looked at us suspiciously. From the cheese department, Jacques continued to shout, "They stole blue cheese! Don't let them get away!"

"Hurry!" I yelled to Emily, who was still waiting outside. "They're after us!"

We tore down Broadway, dodging the pedestrians and book carts. Jacques's keys jingled in my pocket. We'd done it. But now what?

On the corner of Broadway and Seventy-second, we slowed down a little. "We did good," Mariella said. "But I bet he's gonna notice pretty fast that his keys are gone. We don't have much time."

Jason
(aka the hobbit)

We arrived at Jason's building for part two of the plan.

"It's Bulldog!" Emily whispered, pointing. There he was, arms crossed over his chest, bald head gleaming. He caught sight of us and glowered.

But Mariella marched right up to him and pulled her feathery hat down over her eyes. "Hello there, Francis," she said.

Bulldog's face softened. I looked at Emily. *"Francis?"* I said. "His name's *Francis?*"

"Francis, you're looking so buff today!" Mariella cooed, petting Bulldog's shoulder. "You look really muscley!"

I nudged Emily nervously. Uh-oh. Bulldog—er, Francis—might throw her out for that.

But to my surprise, he smiled. "Thank you," he said in a heavy New York accent. "I go to a boxing gym in Brooklyn."

"How wonderful!" Mariella said, tipping back on her heel. "I do tae kwon do! We should spar sometime!"

"This is priceless." Emily nudged me.

"You shoulda seen her in Kaputsa's," I whispered back.

Mariella continued, "So, anyway, we're going up to see Jason Anderson. Seven-L?"

"Of course, I recognize you. Go on up. These two with you?" He motioned to us.

"Yes."

And like that, we were in the building. Mariella led us to the elevator. "That was amazing!" I said.

Mariella rolled her eyes. "That was nothing," she said. But she blushed.

Up on Jason's floor, Mariella strode confidently down the hall and rang the bell for 7-L. Someone opened the door just a crack. "Who is it?"

"It's Mariella, idiot," she answered him. "I *told* you I was gonna come over! Open up!"

"Hold on . . . ," Jason said. He came out into the hall, closing the door behind him. He was super pimply, but he was also tall, had nice brown hair, and wore cool Adidas sneakers.

"So, we got the guy's keys," Mariella said in a low voice.

"Really?" Jason said. "Wow."

"So can you show us where the apartment is?"

"Uh," Jason said. He kept looking back at his closed door.

"We're going to bust him out," I explained. "Obviously."

"Can I help?" he asked. "I can bring Maxwell." He looked at his door again.

"Why do you keep looking at your door?" Mariella asked.

"No reason," Jason said quickly.

"Can't we go into your apartment?"

"Uh . . . ," Jason said.

Mariella frowned. "Listen. If you want to help, we have to go into your apartment."

"Why?" I started, but Mariella shot me a look.

"Who are you hiding in there?" Mariella asked.

"No one," Jason said, but even I could tell he was lying.

Mariella put her hands on her hips. "Let me in," she said.

"Come *on,* Mariella," Jason said. "I'll just get Maxwell and come back out."

"Who's Maxwell?" I asked.

"Who have you got in there?" Mariella said. "Do you have a *girl* in there?" Then, bully that she was, she shoved Jason out of the way and opened the door herself. Jason ran after her, calling, "It's just . . . she's just . . ."

And then Mariella screamed. We all jumped.

"What is *she* doing in here?" she yelled, bursting back into the hall. A small brown-haired girl in a bright yellow skirt and flip-flops followed her.

"We were just playing PlayStation!" Jason said.

"You're *cheating* on me!" Mariella squealed.

I nudged Emily.

"We're not a couple!" Jason said.

Mariella eyed the girl. "Listen. I know tae kwon do. I could use my Flying Snake move on you and pin you to the ground in two seconds flat."

I snorted. This was too silly.

But the girl was terrified. She let out a little *eep* and headed for the elevator. "Tara!" Jason called after her. But the girl kept going.

Mariella looked pleased with herself. "Now, are you going to help us or what?"

Jason sighed loudly but didn't comment. "Let me get Maxwell. Here, Maxwell, here, boy!"

And then it was my turn to freeze and want to run away. An enormous pointy-eared black and brown dog burst into the hall and ran straight for us.

"Puppy!" Emily said. "C'mere!"

I backed into a wall, heart pounding.

Mariella looked at me. "Remember what I said! Don't show him you're afraid."

"I'm . . . ," I started. I was about to say *I'm not*, but then I remembered. I'd told Mariella about my fear the night before. Emily bent down and petted Maxwell. I guess she knew now too.

Emily looked up at me. "It's okay. He's really nice. Here. Let him smell your hand, like this." She put her hand under his nose.

"I can't," I said, shaking my head.

"It's easy," Emily said. "He likes you. Just stick your hand out."

Maxwell leaned against me a little.

"What if he bites me?" I said uneasily.

"He won't. He just wants you to pet him."

"I have him trained to hurt only bad people," Jason explained. "I thought he could help us break out the kidnapped guy."

The dog eyed me. He seemed okay, though I still couldn't pet him. But I didn't run away, either. I just stood very still, hoping he would leave me alone.

Emily came over to me and squeezed my hand.

"You're probably thinking I'm a wimp," I said in a small voice.

"Are you kidding? You're totally not a wimp. Besides, you just stole the Cheese Man's keys!"

"True," I said.

"Okay, bonding moment over," Mariella said, holding Maxwell's leash in her hand. "Let's get this show on the road. I have a manicure at two, and I don't want to be late!"

"Upstairs, then," I said. Maxwell trotted along beside me.

Cheese. Everywhere.

20

"This is his door," Jason said. It was a plain door with a brass knocker. I shivered and felt for the keys in my pocket. They were still covered in blue cheese. I wiped them off on my shirt and found the one that fit the lock.

The door slid open.

"Ew" was Mariella's first word when she stepped inside.

There was cheese everywhere. On the kitchen counter, on the chairs, wrapped in piles on the table. Big wheels of it, little flakes of it in the linoleum and the cracks of the hardwood floor. Even a big barrel of it was in the corner of the kitchen. You could practically see stink vapors wafting around over our heads.

"*Gross,*" Emily said.

Maxwell trotted over to the barrel. "Maxwell!" Jason whispered.

Too late. Maxwell had already stuck his head in the barrel. Gobbling noises followed.

"Ew, he's *eating it!*" Emily said.

"Maxwell!" Jason said. "Maxwell, get out of that cheese barrel!"

But Maxwell wasn't hearing it.

"He does *love* cheese," Jason said.

"Come on," I said. "Let's find James."

"I think this might be the bedroom!" Mariella called. "Except it's locked!"

We ran back to join her. I peered into a room across the hall. It looked like it was the Cheese Man's bedroom. Everything was in perfect order. Several purple and white Kaputsa's uniforms were lying across the bed, neatly pressed. Another hung on the closet door. The walls were lined with shelves, and the shelves were covered in blocks, wheels, braids and triangles . . . of cheese.

Jason jiggled the knob of the closed door and then pointed. "Look, it has a keyhole! Jillian, are there any other keys on his key ring?"

"Well, there's one other one, but Mariella said it goes to some sort of cheese cabinet," I murmured, handing the key ring to him. He tried the other key, but it didn't fit.

We searched an end table in the hall. But all that was

on it was a giant wheel of Gouda. We looked inside the drawers but only found Kaputsa's receipts and a map of Wisconsin. I ran into his bedroom—ugh, what a smell— and looked around on his dresser and desk. I made the mistake of opening his underwear drawer and saw that his underwear was all either Kaputsa's purple and white striped or covered in little pictures of cheese! I shut the drawer fast, gagging. I looked around on his bed and in his bathroom, too, but came up with nothing.

Then we heard a small voice from inside James's room. "Is someone there?"

"Yes, but shhhhh," Emily said.

"Let me try a credit card," Jason said, pulling a card out of his pocket and sliding it between the door and the wall.

"That's not a credit card, big shot, that's a Blockbuster video card!" Mariella argued. "It's not gonna work!"

"Maybe I can bust it down!" Jason said, throwing his shoulder against the door. He winced in pain. "Ow," he said in a wimpy voice.

"Let me try," Mariella said, and gave the door a tae kwon do kick. But it didn't work: it was solid. She grabbed the knob again and frantically shook it. "Open!" she shouted, frustrated.

Suddenly, I remembered something that Mrs. W had told me. "Why don't we try Mrs. W's keys?" I said. I still had them with me. "She told me before she left that some of the Upper West Side buildings have the same locks!"

"That's an urban myth," Mariella said. "Everyone knows that."

"Well, it's worth a shot," Jason said.

He grabbed the keys from me and tried each one in the lock. On the last key, the lock turned. We pushed the door, but it still wouldn't open.

I looked at Mariella. "There must be another lock," I said. "And another key."

"This is taking too long!" Emily said. "The Cheese Man might be on his way back here!"

Mariella shook her head. "We have to try to get the kid inside to help us. Hey, kid!" she called. "Are you there?"

"James!" Emily called.

"Yes?" came the small voice again.

"James, can you unlock the door from the inside?"

"I can only open one of the locks," James called. "But not the second."

"Can you come and try?"

"I don't know if I can walk down the stairs," James said.

I looked at Jason, confused. "Stairs?" I whispered.

"It's a duplex," Jason explained. "Behind that door is a spiral staircase that leads to an upstairs room."

Oh, right. "We're here to rescue you!" I called. "Can you try?"

"Okay . . . ," he said. We heard him slowly creaking down the spiral staircase. It took him almost five minutes, but finally he got to the door. We heard the metallic sound of a lock clicking open. And then the door swung free!

There, in the dim light, was one of the cutest boys I'd ever seen.

I mean, he was a little skinny, and there were dark circles under his eyes, but he was still gorgeous. He looked completely stunned.

"Wow," I said. His eyes were piercingly blue. Emily gripped my arm.

"Hi," the guy finally said. He stared right at me.

"Come on," Mariella said. "We're busting you out!"

"Not so fast," came an icy voice behind us.

Maxwell
(loves cheese)

21

"*S*acre bleu!" the Cheese Man said. "You steal cheese from me, and now you steal him! *Big* mistake!"

He grabbed the back of my neck with one hand and Emily's neck with the other. Emily screamed as he pushed us over to the wall. My leg smashed into the corner of the end table. I crumpled onto the floor.

I could barely breathe, but I struggled to get up. Jason squashed himself into a corner in an attempt to hide. Emily's eyes were closed, and there was a cut on the side of her head. My heart was pounding so hard, I could feel it through my whole body.

The Cheese Man muttered and grunted. The dog started barking, but the Cheese Man didn't seem to notice. Slowly, without turning his back to us, he reached down to open a drawer in a small table in the hall and pulled out a large ball of twine.

"You can be my captives too," he snarled, baring his greenish-yellow teeth. Grunting, he dragged a chair into the middle of the room and picked Emily up and forced her down into it. Then he began to bind her wrists.

I choked on hot tears. I was too petrified to move. Emily whimpered. Jason huddled in the corner, muttering what sounded like a prayer. Mariella was crouched inside the bathroom.

James, weakened by all the activity, lay motionless on the floor.

The Cheese Man finished binding Emily's wrists and ankles. Then he turned and stomped down the hall toward me. He had an evil grin on his face. I let out a small, pathetic little scream, making myself into a tiny ball against the wall.

He was just a few feet from me. Then all of a sudden, I saw Mariella's foot stick out, right in his path. At the last second, he tripped. His twine went flying all over the place and he fell onto the carpet. He was so tall, it was like a tree was falling. I backed out of the way. He landed on the ground with a thud and his eyes rolled back into his head.

And then Mariella climbed on top of him and started punching his face!

She was making the crazy martial arts noises she'd made in her presentation the other night: stuff like *hi-yaah!* and *whoo-hwa!* I covered my mouth. He squealed in pain. Then he rolled over, trying to hit her back. But Mariella was too quick! She sprang up and dodged his punches! My mouth hung open, stunned. The Cheese Man stood, fists flying toward Mariella, but she managed to trip him again with a roundhouse kick right at his ankles.

But then, as Mariella was leaning down to pummel him further, he caught hold of her foot. Down Mariella went with a little whimpering noise. I looked around me. What could I do? What could I do? *WHAT COULD I DO!?* There was a giant wheel of Camembert on the end table. I touched it. It had gone soft—too soft to hurt someone with. I flattened myself against the wall, my heart pounding.

Then I saw my answer.

Maxwell, apparently done eating, had stepped into the hallway.

At first the dog looked incredibly confused. His ears stuck up, and he cocked his head. I could see his big teeth, and there was cheese caked all around his mouth. The mouth that might bite me.

But I had to do it.

"Maxwell," I called in a tiny voice.

The dog's eyes focused on me. My heart thumped.

"Maxwell," I yelled more loudly. I pointed at the Cheese Man, who was beginning to tie Mariella to a very heavy-looking hallway credenza leg. "Maxwell, *sic!*"

And then, miraculously, Maxwell barked and pounced. He landed right on the Cheese Man and sank his giant teeth into the Cheese Man's leg. The Cheese Man howled in pain. Maxwell started shaking his head around, back and forth, his jaws securely on the leg, as if he was trying to separate the Cheese Man's leg from the rest of him.

The Cheese Man let go of Mariella. Maxwell snarled and growled and wouldn't let go. "Get him off, get him off!" the Cheese Man cried, making a series of gurgly noises.

I ran over to untie Mariella, and she wriggled out of the twine and stood. She hovered over the Cheese Man and watched Maxwell shake his head back and forth. Her face was covered in cheese and streaked with blood. But she didn't seem to care. The Cheese Man looked up at her pleadingly.

"Help," he said. There was a smudge of blood on his mustache. "If you get this dog off me, I'll . . . I'll give you free admission to my cheese museum! For life!"

Mariella wrinkled her bloodied nose. "Cheese museum?" she said. "Why in the world would I want to go to a cheese museum?" She rolled her eyes.

"I'm going to build it . . . with my million dollars!" the Cheese Man yelled.

From the bedroom, Mariella grabbed the biggest club of string cheese I'd ever seen. She raised it above her head

like the martial arts sword from her dojo and beane(
Cheese Man.

He was out cold.

"Cheese museum," Mariella muttered, breathing hard.
"That's the stupidest thing I've ever heard."

Maxwell still chewed furiously on the Cheese Man's
leg. "Quick!" Mariella said. "Jillian, get James, there, on
the floor!"

I scurried over to James and bent down. He was
breathing raggedly. "Come on," I whispered. "Can you
stand? Are you strong enough to get out of here?"

"I . . . think," James said. I helped him up. He kept his
eyes gratefully on me the whole time.

"What's your name?" he said weakly.

"Jillian," I said.

"I'm James," he said.

"I know," I said.

He leaned on me and we ran, as fast as James could go,
past the Cheese Man, down the hall.

Jason, who'd gotten back up, untied Emily.
"Maxwell," he called, turning back to the dog. "Maxwell,
heel!"

And just like that, Maxwell released his jaws from the
Cheese Man's leg and trotted over to Jason.

"Gross, the Cheese Man's cheesy blood is all over his
mouth!" Emily said.

"He probably tastes like cheese," Jason said. "That
might've been why Maxwell was so interested in chewing
on him."

"Ew!" I said.

Jason, Mariella, Emily, James, and I staggered out the door, with Maxwell at our side. I shut it tight, hoping that the Cheese Man wouldn't wake up for a long time.

James

22

We were quite a sight. Mariella's face had a big scratch on it, and her arms were turning black and blue. Emily had cuts on her head, wrists, and ankles. I had a big cut on my leg, and Maxwell had cheese and blood all over his face. We snuck past Bulldog when he was on the phone and headed across the street to the Dakota. We needed some advice from Montego.

"What *happened* to you kids?" he said, standing up from his post.

None of us knew how to answer.

He looked at James and shook his head slowly in disbelief. "Hey, you're that kidnapped kid, aren't you?"

James nodded.

"How did you . . . ," Montego said, stunned. "You were . . . where?"

"It's a long story," I said.

"You kids look terrible!" Montego said, putting his hands to his forehead. "I have to sit down for this."

"We just want to get him to a police station," I said. "Where's the closest one?"

"There's one on West Eighty-second Street," Montego murmured. "But why don't I call the police? They can come here, and—"

"We don't want to draw attention to ourselves," I said. The others nodded. "So we'd rather that James went to the police himself."

"Whatever you say," Montego said.

"Thanks," I said, giving his hand a squeeze. "And . . . you won't say anything about this, will you?"

"As usual, Jillian, your secrets are safe with me," Montego said, and winked.

We started uptown to the police station. "You were brilliant with Maxwell," Jason said. "I was too scared to even speak. But he doesn't respond to just anyone's commands. He must've thought you were an authority."

"Really?" I said. I looked down at Maxwell. He hadn't bitten me after all. He'd listened to me. I leaned down, let him sniff me as Emily had instructed, and then started petting his head. It wasn't bad at all. His fur was coarse but warm. He leaned against me and raised his head for more. It was kind of nice.

I had a feeling my dad would be really proud of me.

"So what will James say to the police?" Emily asked. "I mean, if our parents found out we were involved . . ."

"I could say that I escaped Jacques all by myself," James said. "Believe me, I've *wanted* to forever. Especially in the last week or so, when things began to get really stinky."

"Yeah, but the police will see the dog bites on the Cheese Man's leg," I said.

"I could say I was just walking by with my dog," Jason said. "And James flung the door open, and I had my dog attack?"

"You would do that?" Mariella asked.

"Sure," Jason said. "I'll be a hero!"

We all smirked. Jason had been the least brave of any of us.

"Still, you're going to look like a real tough guy in the police station if the police think you beat him up like that all on your own," I said to James. "Jacques is gonna have a lot of bruises on his face when he wakes up."

"Like someone else we know," Mariella said, checking out her reflection in a car mirror. "I guess I'm going to have to say I got beat up pretty bad at the dojo today or something."

"It'll be okay," I said. "I'll cover for you. You were awesome up there. If you hadn't tripped him, he would've tied me up . . . and then . . ."

"We were *all* great up there." Mariella smiled.

We stopped in front of the police station. "Well, this is it," James said weakly. "I don't even know you guys, so . . . thanks for rescuing me. By the way, how did you find out where I was?"

"Oh . . . ," Emily said, giving me a sidelong glance. "Well, we saw you in your room from our apartment building, across the street."

"Wow," James said, pushing back some of his adorably floppy hair. "*Seriously?* I didn't see you. . . ."

"We used binoculars," I admitted, and started giggling.

I shifted from one foot to the other. It was sad to see James go, especially since Emily and I had really come to know him—in a way. And it was too bad, because we'd probably never see him again.

"Can I get your phone number?" James said. "I'm in the city all the time. We can hang out." Maybe I was imagining it, but it seemed like he was looking directly at me when he said it. I blushed.

Mariella had a pen in her bag and passed it to me. I wrote our numbers on an olive leaflet I'd gotten at Kaputsa's. "Here you go," I said shyly.

"All right, you'd better get in there," Emily said, giving him a little shove. James staggered to the door. We crouched down, waiting. As soon as James walked in, about five cops swarmed around him. They'd all seen his picture on the news, after all.

We waited and watched. James seemed to be telling them the story of how he'd escaped from the Cheese Man.

Someone was taking notes. They led James into a back room. Someone got on the phone.

Seconds later, a bunch of cops ran out of the station, piled into six cop cars, and went screaming toward Seventy-second Street.

"Wow," I said. "That was quick."

"Do you think he'll be okay?" Emily said.

"Sure," Jason said. "*Anything's* better than being in that Cheese Man's apartment!"

"He's got a point," Mariella said.

"You know, I'm starving," I said. "Is there anywhere good to eat around here?"

After stopping at home and cleaning up our wounds, we headed back out onto the street. "I know a good place for burgers," Mariella said. "Just a few blocks up."

We traipsed up to Jackson Hole, which Mariella said was famous for its hamburgers. I was afraid it was going to be some super-trendy, expensive place, but to my surprise, it was friendly and really comfortable. They even gave Maxwell a bowl of water and some bones. We were all still kind of freaked out, but for some reason we all had enormous appetites. All of us—including Mariella, who typically ate only salads—ordered giant burgers. We even got *cheese* on our burgers.

"This cheese looks a little like Velveeta," Mariella said, and burst out laughing.

"This is delicious," I said. "Maybe the best burger I've ever had."

"See, New York isn't so bad, is it?" Mariella said. "We actually have *edible* food here."

"It's true," I said.

"There are a lot of fun things to do here, you know," Mariella said. "The boats in Central Park, the Cyclone at Coney Island, the shopping on Madison Avenue, walking around SoHo . . ."

"Will you take me?" I blurted out. I'd always wanted to go on the Cyclone. My dad and I used to love going on roller coasters together. We never screamed on the hills, though. Instead we laughed crazily while waving our hands up in the air.

Mariella blinked. "Sure," she said. "That would be nice. I'll take both you and Emily. Like a big sister."

I thought about rolling my eyes at "big sister," but I smiled instead. Next to my dad, Mariella and Emily seemed like good friends to ride a roller coaster with.

"And Jillian," Mariella said, "maybe you can give me some art lessons." She turned to Jason. "Jillian is an *amazing* artist. It was because of her sketch that we figured out the kidnapper was the Cheese Man!"

My mouth fell open. Mariella *liked* my artwork? "Thanks," I squeaked.

"Oh my god, look," Jason said, pointing at the door. We all turned, panicked, thinking it was the Cheese Man. But instead, it was just an anonymous person with a purple and white striped Kaputsa's bag slung over her shoulder. I thought about the purple and white striped underwear and half gagged, half laughed.

"I never want to see purple and white stripes again," Emily said.

"Me neither," I agreed.

How could I have
forgotten??

23

"**H**ave you heard the news?" my mother asked as I walked back into my apartment. "That kidnapped boy has been found!"

"Really," I said. I tried to sound as nonchalant as possible. It was six o'clock; I was planning to pretend I'd been at camp all day.

"Yes, he was in the building across the street!" my mother exclaimed.

The TV was showing James being reunited with his

parents. And there was live coverage of Jason and Maxwell being interviewed by a TV reporter!

"I just happened to be walking by the man's apartment, and I saw what was going on, and I sent my dog into the apartment to help!" Jason said, smiling.

"I'm *so* relieved he's been found and that horrible kidnapper is off the streets!" my mother said, putting a hand to her forehead. "It's so scary to think he was *so close*! You kids were in *danger*!"

"Have they said who the kidnapper was yet?" I asked innocently.

"They haven't released his name," my mother said.

Then she looked at me. Her eyes widened. "*Jillian!* What happened to your *leg*? There's a giant gash on it!"

"Yeah," I said. "Camp-related accident. Field day."

"Goodness, between your leg and someone accidentally punching Mariella at tae kwon do, it's been a very violent day!"

I looked at Mariella, who was sitting in an easy chair with an ice pack on her cheek, and winked.

The television showed James eating a big sandwich and smiling for the camera. His famous senator father shook Jason's hand and patted Maxwell on the head.

"My, my." My mother inspected my leg more closely. "I thought this was an arts camp!"

"They like us to be active," I said.

"Well, it's a good thing that today was your last day!" my mother said.

Last day? Could it be . . . ? I quickly counted back the

weeks. Wow. It *was* my last day. Today was the last week of July, just when camp was scheduled to end. I couldn't believe my luck.

And better yet: school didn't start for another month. I had all of August to explore this crazy city.

"Let me get some bacitracin for that cut," my mother said, walking out of the room.

"Go, you," Mariella whispered from across the room. "Last day of camp!"

"Yeah," I laughed. "Who knew?"

home at the Dakota

The next day, I found Emily waiting at Mrs. W's apartment. We both spoke at the same time. "You'll never believe this," Emily said.

"I have the best news!" I said.

"You first," she said.

"Camp is over!" I said. "I don't ever have to go back!"

Emily started laughing. "You're kidding," she said. "That's what I was gonna tell you! My camp ended yesterday too!"

"Awesome," I said. "We're free!"

Once we were inside Mrs. W's apartment, we went over to the window and looked across the street. James's window was now dark. "I still can't believe it happened," Emily said quietly.

I nodded. Instead of watching James from across the street, we watched him on the news instead. First, there was the same footage from before: James eating the sandwich, Jason's statement, James's father patting Maxwell on the head.

"Jason's gonna be a huge hero," Emily said.

"And Maxwell is going to be a star," I said.

But then the newscaster said they had breaking news: the name of the kidnapper!

The camera switched to an image of the Cheese Man, his leg wrapped in bandages, being led out of his apartment building by the police. They didn't give much background on him, saying only that he was a strangely quiet employee of Kaputsa's cheese department and apparently had an obsession with cheese.

A Kaputsa's employee came on the screen. Underneath her face was her name: AMANDA LOPEZ, CHECKOUT CLERK. "Jacques was acting very strange this morning," she said. "He was yelling crazily that a customer had stolen cheese. And then he ran out of the store, abandoning his cheese counter, which he never does. We *knew* something was up."

"You can say that again," I said.

"Hello?" A voice rang out behind us. Emily and I both jumped. It was Mrs. W, returning from her trip. She had about a million bags in her hands. I rushed up to help her with them.

"Remember me?" she asked merrily.

"Of course!" I said. "How was your trip?"

"Oh, lovely, lovely. Where's my Mipsy?"

She hunted around for the cat for a few minutes and found her at her scratching post. She cradled the cat in her arms and walked back into the living room, where we were still watching coverage of the kidnapping. Mrs. W looked tanned and rested—and there was a streak of pink dye in her hair.

"I heard there was big news while I was gone! A kidnapping!"

"Yeah," Emily said.

"I can't believe it, a kidnapping right across the street from us!" Mrs. W said. "Why, I remember we had last year's Christmas party in that building! Remember that, Emily? Oh, that was a lovely one. I think I have pictures of it somewhere."

I smirked at Emily behind Mrs. W's back.

Mrs. W flopped down on the couch and put her hand over her head. We all watched the TV in silence. There was the Cheese Man again, being led into the police station. You could hear him muttering something about an expensive barrel of cheese being eaten. We could hear him say, "Horrible dog," and "My precious cheese, all gone!"

"What is he talking about?" Mrs. W said, straining to hear.

"A dog ate all his precious cheese," Emily said, and immediately clapped her hand over her mouth.

"A . . . a *what?*" Mrs. W said.

Emily didn't answer, and we could hardly contain ourselves and keep from giggling. I wondered if I could tell Mrs. W the whole James adventure some day. I bet I could. She'd probably get a kick out of it. Besides, it's no fun having an adventure that you can't share with a couple of people.

"Oh, girls," Mrs. W sighed, turning down the volume of the television. "It's been hard being out of the city. You always miss something fascinating!"

"It's true," I said.

She eyed me carefully. "So, did you have a good month?"

"I did," I said, and smiled. "I . . . I made some friends. And did a lot of exciting stuff!"

"Good." Mrs. W sighed. "So that means you like New York City now?"

"I think I do." I smiled. "I believe I'll stay."

ABOUT THE AUTHOR

Natalie Fast sketches, likes cake, hates cheese, and has survived camp. She lives in New York City but not, unfortunately, in the Dakota.